LUCKY ROCKS

Murray Richter

Ten Story Books, LLC
Dallas, TX

Published by Ten Story Books, LLC
P.O. Box 701561, Dallas, TX 75370

Ten Story Books, LLC and the Ten Story Books logo are
trademarks of Ten Story Books, LLC

ISBN-10: 0991634888
ISBN-13: 978-0-9916348-8-0

Library of Congress Control Number: 2014944974

Cover design by Nathan Reinhardt
http://nathanr.carbonmade.com/

Cover photos:
© Erico | Dreamstime.com
© Luhuanfeng | Dreamstime.com
© Hanhanpeggy | Dreamstime.com
© Michael Mill | Dreamstime.com

First edition: September, 2014

Summary: From relentless pranks to monster fish, Kevin, Rudy, and Preech
experience the summer of a lifetime.

Thank you for purchasing this Ten Story Books, LLC publication.
www.tenstorybooks.com

To Grandma, Grandpa, Mama K and Papa,
four of the smartest people to have
ever walked the planet.
I just wish I'd have figured it out sooner.

CHAPTER 1

If I didn't get a hook in the water soon, my head was going to explode. But there were two small problems—the little munchkin and a pile of chores.

My little sister, Milly, was four and did kooky things all the time. She made (and sometimes tasted) triple-decker mud pies and talked to dragonflies. Today, however, she was bent on getting entertained by me and my best friends, Preech and Rudy.

"We're working on something very important. Why don't you try to catch your shadow?" I pleaded.

"I tried Kevin, really really hard. But it's too slippery."

Milly pulled at my shirt and started singing something about a game of hopscotch or ring around the whatever, and I glanced at Preech and Rudy for help. They acted like they were focused on tying the fishing poles to their bikes. We'd geared up for fishing about a million times before, and it looked like the poles were secure enough to make a ride across Alaska.

"All right, all right, let's go find something to do. I'll meet you two in the house in a minute."

Preech nodded, "Ten-four, see you there." As he bent over to give Milly a high five, Rudy gave him a wedgie that lifted Preech so high his toes barely touched the ground.

I laughed and watched Preech chase Rudy into the house. He shook a fist at Rudy with one hand as he pulled his underwear out with the other.

I put Milly on my shoulders as we walked towards the flower bed surrounded by monkey grass. The begonias stood at attention like little soldiers, and the elephant ear plants had leaves as big as Milly. The names of the plants were burned into my brain because I was the "chosen one" to replant new ones each spring since they all died at some point every summer.

I'd get thrown around behind our six-hundred-year-old tiller to turn in new dirt, which made my teeth feel like they were rattling out of their sockets, then I'd put the plants into their new homes. I felt sad I was sending them to their death, but maybe our backyard was the place plants were sent to kick the bucket.

I didn't know what the big deal was about flowers and plants because they really didn't do anything. But aloe vera was different. It rubbed out a sunburn and took the sting out of my scorched fingers once when I accidentally held a firecracker too long.

"Hey look, there's one," I said as I set her down and pointed at the long green strands of grass.

"Mini-monkeys? Really?" Milly squealed as she bent over to get a closer look.

"Yep, that's why they call it monkey grass. He jumped into the shadows. Just sit as still as a stick, and they'll come back out in a few minutes."

"How little are they?" she whispered.

"As little as a roly poly, but they can see a penny on the moon and hear toilet paper tear five blocks away. So you gotta be real still and extra quiet."

Some guilt crept up on me, but I pushed it aside because we had to get to the pond before it got too hot and the fish stopped biting. The guilt didn't stab me as hard as it did a few weeks ago, when as a joke, I taught her that "on purpose" meant "on accident."

Man did she get in trouble for breaking mom's lamp on purpose.

"When'll the monkeys come back?"

"Just stay real still, and say your ABCs in your head ten times in a row. Then they should come out. Just stay still. And don't forget to breathe."

I patted her on the head then backed up, watching her mouth her ABCs and bug her eyes out as she stared at the monkey grass.

Back at the house I opened the door to the laundry room and grabbed a wire coat hanger as I passed through. Rudy and Preech were in the den, ready for action. We eased down the hallway towards mom's door, until Rudy started giggling like a hyena.

I turned around to see him elbow Preech as he pointed at my sixth grade picture from last year. Both of my eyes were closed, and my mouth was half-opened. It was kind of funny, but the two of them laughed way too hard every time they looked at it.

It was good to see Rudy smile again. Things were getting ugly with his stepdad, Ted, and I swore to myself I would figure out a way to help him. After going fishing, of course.

Preech was as smart as most men I knew, and Rudy was almost as tall and had as much body hair as most men, and I was kind of left in the dust. I hoped there was some way I would catch up, but the call of a perfect fishing day scrambled my brain. We had to focus and make our getaway.

"Shh, don't you know moms hear through walls?"

"Sorry Buddy," Preech whispered through his massive grin. "Why don't we just ask her if we can go fishin'?"

"Well, do you think the fish are bitin' right now, right this second?"

They both nodded.

"Do you think they will be bitin' in a few hours after all my chores get done?"

They both shook their heads.

"So we've gotta figure out a way to go fishin' when they're bitin'. Chores can wait. The fish won't. Hey, you guys are going to help me with the chores when we get back, right?"

"Oh, yeah, sure," said Preech.

"Can't wait," whispered Rudy.

Yeah right, I thought, but knew I could lure at least one of them back with a promise to play on my new Atari game after the chores were knocked out.

The fluffy new carpet cushioned my knees as I crouched down and put my head against mom's bedroom door. The color of the carpet was called avocado green and sea foam blue, something mom told me over and over because we needed to take care of it so it would "last a lifetime." It looked more like bluegill green and catfish blue to me, but my dad always said "a happy wife is a happy life" so he bought some for every room but the garage.

It was 1979, and my mom thought that soon we'd have hovercrafts instead of cars. Once that happened, she'd get carpet for the garage and her world would be complete.

"Okay guys, I watched her finish her second cup of coffee earlier. Once we hear the bathroom door close, it's go time."

It felt like a hundred days drug by until we finally heard the bathroom door click shut.

I silently counted on my fingers to ten, then straightened out the top of the coat hanger. I eased it into the hole on the lock of the bedroom door until the metallic pop told us the door was unlocked. We peeked inside and saw nothing, then tiptoed like ninjas across the room to the bathroom door.

I smiled and nodded at Preech and Rudy, then slipped the coat hanger into the lock.

The lock clicked open and we burst into the bathroom and found a very surprised mom on the commode.

"Can we go fishing? Please?! They've got to be biting!" We all talked at once, and it was deafening. Rudy and Preech had their eyes pinched shut so they wouldn't see anything they didn't want to.

"What? Get out of here! Go!" she shot back as she covered herself with her magazine.

CHAPTER 2

We ran through the house, jumped down the back steps, and grabbed our bikes.

Milly ran and skidded to a stop in front of the back gate, holding her arms out and blocking our escape.

"The monkeys must be sleepin'. What y'all wanna do now?"

Preech and Rudy chewed nervously on their bottom lips as they looked back towards the house. I eased Milly aside with one hand and jerked the gate lock open with the other.

"Must be monkey nap time, which is something you need to do. Like right now."

"I ain't sleepy. Whatcha wanna do?"

She grinned her mile-wide grin and batted her eyelashes at me, something I normally couldn't say no to. But that day we had poked the dragon, and there was no turning back.

"Oh man, I think I saw her shadow in the window. She's coming man." Preech stuttered as he looked back and forth from me to the house.

"Listen Little Monkey, we really need to get going. How 'bout I promise to play whatever game you want when I get back?"

"Nope."

"How 'bout a dollar?" blurted Preech. He hardly ever spent money, which is probably why he always had more than Rudy and me.

"A whole dollar?" beamed Milly.

"Yep, take it, please." Preech crammed his hand into his pocket then thrust the wadded bill at Milly.

I bent over to look her in the eyes—our noses almost touched. "Now you better run inside and stick that in your piggy bank. Mini-monkeys can steal money almost as good as they can see."

With that she took off to the house, and we pedaled as fast as we could out of the back gate and down the alley. We stood on our pedals and rode like the wind until it felt like we were out of earshot from the house. Then we eased into our seats and started coasting.

"You know, it might be easier to just plan fishing in advance and work around the other stuff," panted Preech.

"I know, I know, but every now and then a perfect fishing day jumps up out of nowhere and we gotta go. There will always be chores."

There was a sound like a piece of tape being torn from cardboard box, and I figured Preech's legs were starting to stick to his blue banana seat. It was still morning, but the heat was setting in and his legs made the sound every time his foot rose with the pedal.

Rudy must have heard it too, because he laughed and said, "You know, if you had a manlier bike, or manlier legs, you wouldn't sound like a broken vacuum going down the street." Preech swerved at Rudy, which caused Rudy to swerve and smack against a curb.

But Rudy didn't wipe out. He had better balance than anyone I knew. If I hit a pebble in the road it seemed like I'd do a thousand flips, but Rudy was ice-cold cool.

Preech had some balance issues too, but nothing like me. He was also the smartest kid in our class, and if he didn't know the answer for something, he knew how to find it fast.

There were other friends at school and around town, but Preech and Rudy were the best. Preech helped keep Rudy from failing classes, and Rudy kept me from getting beat up.

We took a short cut down an alley and popped out on the edge of town. After about a half a mile alongside the highway, we turned onto the dirt road that led to the pond.

"I'm sure glad you didn't get grounded for ruining your dad's barbeque pit, Kev man. Some experiments just don't work out," said Preech.

"Me too. For the first time in my life I just told him I did it and didn't blame the cat or aliens. He said it was good that I was headin' in the right direction, and I shouldn't get any more whippin's if I continue to take things like a man." Both my mom and dad would say things about me becoming a man, but I sure didn't look or feel like one.

Preech smacked his lips. "Is he gettin' a new pit? His redfish on the half shell is the best thing I've ever put in my mouth."

"I told him if he did I'd pay him back with the money I make mowing and doing the other jobs people ask me to. I also promised I'd pay him back for the lighter fluid, but I'm not gonna touch another bottle of that stuff for as long as I live."

Preech smiled and squinted towards the pond. A small strip of the water crept into sight. Like always, we sprinted the last hundred yards to the end of the road. And like always, Rudy let us get ahead of him a ways then blew past us.

Rudy skidded to a stop just as he hit the grass, and Preech waited till the last second and skidded to a sideways stop on the dusty road just before it reached the grass. Pebbles and dust flew up from his tires, wrapping Rudy in a tiny dirt storm.

"Nice job, slick," said Rudy as he spit and blinked his eyes clean.

"Ha, I let you win because I knew that someday you'd stop right there to gloat. You may be as big as a yeti, and smell like one, but your lack of brains helps me stay eons ahead."

I took a deep breath and looked out over the pond. The air had the thick, sweet taste of summer, and I felt as free as a bird. People from out of town said our summer air was like breathing through cloth, but we loved it.

The pond was about as big as five football fields. Half of the pond had cattails along the shore, and a mysterious tree-covered island in the middle. The island was about the size of ten school buses mashed together and doubled its size when the rains didn't come.

I arched my eyebrows and asked, "Do y'all want to try to swim to the island and fish it today? There's gotta be huge fish that ain't ever seen a hook swimmin' around there right this second."

"I do, I really do," answered Preech, "but I still couldn't get a straight answer if water moccasins can bite under water. I asked the vet, a policeman, and my dad and they didn't know. And all the books I read at the library told me everything about snakes except for if they can bite under water. I'll keep workin' on it though."

As we walked to the edge of the pond, I watched startled frogs burp their discontent and dive into the coffee-colored water. Baitfish swirled everywhere, an excellent sign that the bite was on.

Preech shielded his eyes from the sun with his hand and looked at the pond. "There's gotta be a way to capture and use indigenous fish for bait. I just don't know how to get 'em."

"Ohh, there you go again, Alfred Einstein," Rudy muttered. "I swear you just sit around and make up words."

Preech shook his head. "No, it was actually the word for yesterday in the word-of-the-day calendar I got at home."

"That's messed up in so many ways," sighed Rudy "Did you ever check to make sure the guy who wrote that wasn't drunk or something? Or it's not some joke book with words that aren't even real? Half of the words you say make you sound like a Klingon."

"That's what word of the day toilet paper is for," answered Preech, and we all busted out laughing.

"So, how do you reckon we get some of those indigestion fish? Do they sell them at the bait shop?" Rudy asked.

"No, the real name is actually, umm, I mean, you're right. It is indigestion fish. Make sure you use that in a paper at school and you'll do great. It means they are from a particular area or live in a certain place, like the minnows and small perch that live in the water here. I've drawn up some plans for a big basket net thing to catch them with, but I can't figure out how to make it work."

I smiled and slapped him on the back. "If anyone can, you can, Preech, my man."

Some days we would stop at the bait shack and buy bait and tackle. It was really just a guy that grew worms in a box, sold frozen minnows in plastic bags, and made dough bait out of the stinkiest things on earth. He sold them out of his home, and I could only dream about being so lucky someday. The only problem was it was way on the other side of town. That morning had been a little crazy, and I forgot to think about it.

Rudy pulled the big rocks up next to the pond, and I reached underneath to grab worms to put in our bait can. Preech eased through the weeds and hunted grasshoppers. He was great at catching them and was even better when they were covered with dew. He called dew "earth sweat," something else that cracked me up every time he said it.

After half an hour, our can was full of worms and Preech's jar was packed with grasshoppers and crickets. Preech and Rudy attached bobbers, but something told me to fish on the bottom. I put a worm and a cricket on my hook (I had never double-baited with different kinds of bait) and zinged it as far as I could towards the island.

We sat on the grass and laid back against the rocks, waiting for the mayhem to begin. Mayhem was one of Preech's words for the day a few weeks ago, and it was so fun to think or say I used it every chance I could.

Rudy stood up and walked into the weeds, to go to the bathroom I guessed. "Well Preech my man, I guess our mission for the summer is to get to that island and fish it all day long. Are you in?"

"Heck yeah. I just need to figure out a few things to get us there." Preech dropped his voice to a whisper. "And another thing is figure out what we can do to help Rudy with Ted. I've heard he is turning loco."

"I've been hearin' stuff too, but Rudy won't talk at all about it. When I try to say anything about Ted he just clams up and walks away."

"Same with me. I can build and fix a lot of stuff, but I ain't got nothin' when it comes to families...especially parents. Rudy acts normal when Ted is gone to work on the oil rigs, but when he comes back Rudy changes. And I think it's gettin' worse."

"Me too. When Rudy gets them scratches and bruises on him, he says they're from playin' football, but I'm scared that it might be—" I stopped talking when I heard Rudy coming back.

"You know fellas, I think the coolest super power would be invisibility," said Rudy. "We could walk right in the middle of practice for a football team we're gonna play and figure out what they're good at and not good at. Then we'll tell Coach, put together a perfect game plan, and they'll never know what hit 'em."

Football was Rudy's "thing." Outside of messing with Preech, it was probably all he thought about. He was by far the best athlete in our class and couldn't wait for our first year of real football with pads and everything. People were even talking about us winning some games this year, which was a pretty tall order since that hadn't happened since I was born.

"How 'bout you Kev?"

"I think mind reading would be the best. I can zone in on chicks' brain waves to finally figure them out, and use it on teachers to find out when the next dang pop quiz is coming up. I'd tell y'all for free, but sell it to everyone else to help pay for bait and dad's new barbeque pit."

"I think time travel would be the coolest," said Preech. "I could go back in time and meet Jesus, Ben Franklin, and my all-time favorite, Abraham Lincoln. I read that he wasn't even the main speaker when he did the Gettysburg Address, so I just know I'd be able to get a front row seat. Then I'd travel to the future to terrorize you in the old-folks home or loony bin," he smiled as he pointed at Rudy. "I'm sure you'll be in one or the other, or some monks will probably have to build a special one just for you."

Religion was Preech's "thing." He loved everything about church and had read the Bible all the way through. Most everyone went to church, but Preech loved every second and went to all the extra meetings and services they would come up with.

I guess my "thing" was fishing. I could fish every second of every minute of every hour for my whole life and still not get enough.

"You know, I think we should become fishers of men. We catch 'em, God'll clean 'em," grinned Preech.

"How 'bout you pray you can walk on water while I push you in," answered Rudy. Rudy went to church as well, but I think it was mostly to get away from Ted.

I was about to laugh when my pole jerked out of my hand and sailed towards the water. It bounced off a rock, then disappeared into the murky darkness. Without thinking, I jumped in after it.

CHAPTER 3

The water was surprisingly cool, and I knew it would be dark as night so I didn't even try to open my eyes. I groped along the algae covered rocks on the bottom of the pond until my lungs ached, desperate to find my favorite pole. Something slithered around my ankle and sunk its teeth into me, and I shot up out of the water.

An old lady shriek flew out of my mouth. "Snake, snake, snake!" I tried to blink the water out of my eyes to figure out which way to go.

I heard Preech and Rudy yelling for me, and noticed they were already waist-deep in the water. They had jumped in to help, reason number ten thousand and two why they were my best buddies.

"It's got my leg!"

My ankle burned from the bite. It was trying to pull me backwards so hard I wondered if it was a gator or a snake. I'd never heard of gators that lived around there.

"We got you, man," said Preech as he grabbed my arm. "Let's get you back on the dirt. I've got my snakebite kit. You'll be all right." Preech's snakebite kit was a weird suction cup with wires hooked to it he kept attached to his bike.

Preech and Rudy were wide-eyed as they pulled my arms and looked around for other snakes that might come after us. They leaned over and drug me towards the bank, doing their best to keep their feet as far as they could from mine. We got into shallow water, and I pulled my leg out. What I expected to see was a thirty-foot

13

snake with his ten-inch fangs poking through my ankle. Instead, it was fishing line wrapped around my leg. I had somehow gotten tangled in the line, and the bite I'd felt was the line that had sliced into my skin.

I peeled the line from my ankle, and a drop of blood oozed down into my soggy shoe. I pulled the line as fast as I could, and the tip of my pole emerged from the pond like a submarine periscope. The rest of the pole followed, and I grabbed the handle on the reel and brought the line in as fast as it would come. Even a kindergartener knew that slack in the line gives a fish an excuse to spit the hook.

Whatever monster that had bit was still hooked, and my Zebco reel screamed as the rest of the line was sucked out of it. The pole bent like a pretzel, and I thought it was going to snap.

Rudy's mouth hung open. "That's gotta be a fifty point fish. I've never seen a pole bend like that. Fight 'em Kev man, fight 'em."

There was a point system we'd set up for fishing. Preech and Rudy always came up with reasons to give me points, and ways to take points away from each other. They agreed I had about eight hundred points, but they disagreed on each other's scores. Preech thought Rudy had a score of about a negative two thousand points for doing things like casting like a monkey, and Rudy thought Preech's score was a little lower for doing things like reeling like a sloth.

I glanced at Preech. His eyes were flying back and forth from my ankle to the end of my pole.

"I've got Bactine and bandages on my bike, Amigo. Just get that sucker in and we'll get your leg fixed up."

Preech had read the entire Boy Scout handbook, and was the most prepared person I knew. His bike looked more like a homeless man's shopping cart with his things hanging all over it, but he seemed to always have what we needed.

I wrestled the fish in some and let it pull line back out for what felt like an hour. Each time it took line out the beast lost some energy, and I was able to pull it a little closer before it took another run.

When the pencil-sized dorsal fin finally broke the water, I saw what could have been the biggest catfish in the county.

"That's as big as a dog," hollered Preech. "It's gotta be some kind of record."

I knew a fish that big could probably rip my arm off, so figured I'd better not grab him by the lip to pull him out. Instead, I stepped into the water and reached for his gills. As my fingers brushed his smooth gray skin, he got one more surge of energy. His huge tail flapped, his body turned, then with a final burst he straightened out my hook and took off. I think he stopped for a split second to moon me, but then he was long gone.

"Nooooo," I croaked, and sunk to my knees.

The bubble trail the giant catfish made showed me his escape route. He took off straight for the island.

A memory from a few weeks earlier roared back and socked me in the stomach. We were at the bait shop, and in my infinite (another one of Preech's words for the day) wisdom, I bought the cheap hooks instead of the expensive hooks. It was a difference of fifty-nine cents. At the time I thought saving the money to buy two candy bars instead of one was the smartest business move I could make. Suddenly it felt like the worst decision I would ever make for the rest of my life.

Preech and Rudy sat and watched me in silence for a while, then got into an argument about how many points I should get for doing something so incredible.

"Thanks guys, but I didn't land him so there can't be any points."

Preech helped me back up then opened his first aid kit. "Just fightin' something that big for so long has to count for somethin'."

"And having to stand next to Preech and smell his dragon breath for so long should double the points, kinda like combat pay." Rudy grinned as he shook the last few drops of water out of my reel.

We always threw the fish we caught back in the water to get bigger, but that one was special. "Naw, thanks anyways, but it wouldn't be right if I didn't get it in. I was hopin' to take it back to mom to smooth things over when we get back."

My mom was one of the coolest birds in town. As long as we did our chores and behaved, she'd let us do just about anything. It felt like the big fish getting away may have had something to do with how we sprung ourselves from having to do chores.

Preech poured some red gunk on my ankle, wrapped it with a white cloth, and attached it with Band-Aids. "Maybe you can pick her some flowers on the way home. My dad always brings flowers when he messes up. And so something like this never happens again, I'm going to get to work on a harpoon shooter."

I laughed and looked at the water. "Maybe we can try to catch some of the fish you were talking about for bait. The big fella may be too hook smart to bite a worm and cricket double-baiter again, but maybe we can fool him with a fish he sees all the time."

Preech found the smallest hook he had and gave it to me.

"Maybe this will work if we use just a piece of a worm or cricket for the little fish to bite. If anyone can catch the biggest and littlest fish in the pond on the same day, it's you, Kev man."

I fished for small fish for a couple of hours. My bait got stolen a lot, but I never hooked one. Preech and Rudy also tried to catch bait for a while, then switched back to regular hooks and bait. Preech caught six bass, three catfish, and a turtle. Rudy only landed three bass and a water snake, so according to Preech he lost another fifty points for such wimpy fishing.

I spit into the water and watched the ripples chase each other. "Once my Gramps got a fishing hook so deep in his finger he had to use pliers to get it out. It was too deep to pull out, so he pushed it all the way through, snipped off the barb, then pulled it out."

"Ouch," winced Preech. "Did he spray it with Bactine and Monkey Blood, then wrap it in a sterile cloth?"

"Nope. It squirted some blood into the water and he said, 'That'll bring them suckers in.' Then he tore off a piece of his undershirt to wrap it up and we caught all kinds of fish. He knew more about fishing in his big toe than I'll ever know."

I looked at the sky and could almost feel him watching us. "Man, do I miss him."

"I read somewhere that when an old person dies it's like a library burning up," said Preech.

"When Gramps died it was like a library and a tackle shop burning up." I sighed and looked at the sun, which was sitting right on top of us.

"Well, I guess we'd better start headin' back. I'm pretty sure my chores didn't do themselves."

Preech started to re-attach everything to his bike. "So, do you think your mom's gonna be a little mad like 'waiter, there's a fly in my chili', or real mad like my dad was when we were little and used rocks to play tic-tac-toe on the side of his truck?"

"You never know. I'm pretty sure we'll get the 'don't do the crime if you can't do the time' speech, and after that we'll see. The fishing was awesome though, wasn't it?"

Rudy nodded. "That had to be the biggest fish in the state, possibly the country. We could have put every fish we caught in it and still had room."

I wanted to ask Rudy if things were getting any better with Ted but knew it wouldn't go anywhere. Lately when I'd ask, all he would do was clam up and walk away. Preech and I knew something bad was going on. It frustrated me that we didn't know how to help. If I figured that out, I wondered if I'd take a giant step towards becoming a man.

Rudy and I waited for Preech to get everything roped and tied back on his bike, then pointed for home.

As we pedaled down the dusty road, Rudy smiled and looked at Preech. "You know, this year before football practice starts we all have to get physicals. Full physicals, if you know what I mean."

Preech's eye started to twitch a little, something he did when he got nervous. "No way. I thought that was for eighth grade and above. You sure?"

"Yep. Heard it from Coach. They're gonna start with seventh graders this year. You have to strip naked as a jaybird, then they pull and poke on everything and make you cough. And I do mean everything."

Preech took his hands off of the handlebars for a split second to scratch his head. "But how do I cough while I'm screaming?"

Rudy laughed as we watched a squirrel run across the road in front of us. "I wonder how quick we'll set the all-time record for touchdowns."

I wondered if I would even make the team.

As Rudy pedaled ahead, Preech rode close to me and whispered, "Hey, do you think it would be better for me to put itching powder or cinnamon oil in Rudy's jock strap? You think it'll explode if I put both in there?"

I shrugged and laughed. It amazed me how their brains were wired to prank each other no matter what was going on.

We pulled up to Ken's, a store where we always stopped on the way home. As I slid my kickstand into place, I saw Preech digging furiously through his pockets.

"Everything cool?"

"Yes, well no, well dangit. I swore I had an extra dollar today. I hope it didn't float out in the water."

"I thought that's what was buggin' you. Do you remember everything that happened today?"

"Well, I got up, counted my money, put some in my pants, went to your house...oh, yeah. Milly fleeced me for it."

"Bingo." I grinned. "But thanks to your quick thinkin', we got out of there and dodged the full force of Hurricane Mom. How much money you got?"

Preech stared at the coins in his hand. "About enough for half a Coke."

I saw Rudy counting a handful of pennies. "How 'bout you Rudy?"

"'Bout the same. Do you wanna buy one and split it, Preech?"

Preech stuck his hand out to Rudy. "Deal."

We bought our Cokes and walked back outside. I set the bottle cap on the lip of a brick and karate chopped it open. We could have used the opener attached to the fridge inside the store, but chopping it open was way cooler.

Rudy did the same, then he stepped behind Preech.

Preech looked at me and smacked his forehead. "Oh, I forgot to tell you but someone dumped a bathtub in the ditch by my house. I think it would be the perfect thing to start our own worm farm. And we can grow big ones, like Canadian night crawlers."

I listened to Preech, but something Rudy was doing behind him caught my eye. Rudy's head was all the way back, and he poured the Coke into his mouth as fast as it would go.

"Canadians are super expensive, and if we could grow a lot, I think we could use some and sell some," Preech continued.

I tried as hard as I could to listen to Preech, but after a while I couldn't help it. Something about Rudy's eyes bugging out as the last of the Coke disappeared cracked me up.

Rudy reeled off a huge burp and jumped on his bike. As Preech turned to look, Rudy tossed the empty bottle to him. Preech juggled it a few times then secured it.

"My half was on the bottom, sucker," smiled Rudy as he gained speed and peeked over his shoulder to see if Preech was coming after him. He looked back and slammed on his brakes before he hit a truck that had just pulled in to the parking lot.

A big, loud, dirty truck.

Ted's truck.

My stomach tightened and my spit dried up. I was scared what Ted would do to Rudy for almost hitting his truck. The window rolled down, and Rudy's mom, Daisy, poked her head out and waved at us. Her wavy black hair spilled out over the door handle, and her honey-colored eyes glinted in the sun. I wondered how someone so pretty could be married to such a Neanderthal (another one of Preech's words of the day).

"Hi boys. Hey Rudy honey, you need to come back to the house and help me with a few things. Ted will be back from the rig a few days early, and we need to have everything done by the time he gets back."

"But Mom, I promised Kevin to help out with some of his chores today. Besides, we kinda pulled a fast one to go fishin'. I think I better apologize to his mom."

Daisy's face pinched into a scowl. "You did what?"

"Long story Mom. Let's just say we kinda bent the rules a little. Nobody was hurt or died or anything. I'll tell you later."

"Well, an apology can never wait, so you will call her from the house. Do you want to be the one to tell Ted that you had to do Kevin's chores instead of getting everything around our house done?"

Rudy swallowed hard and shook his head.

"Maybe we can get everything knocked out quick, and you can run over and help Kevin finish his chores. I really don't want to have a repeat of last time when we didn't have everything done and ready when Ted came back...do you?"

Rudy shook his head harder and stared at the parking lot. He glanced back at us, shrugged, and pointed his bike towards his house.

"Sorry about the chores, Kev man. I'll help next time." His voice trailed off as he pedaled away.

Then Rudy pulled up his handlebars and we watched him pop a wheelie for a whole block. It looked so easy for him, like he could do one all day.

I smiled and looked at Preech. "Man is he good at wheelies. I bet he could do one for a mile."

"Yep, prob'ly so," muttered Preech.

Neither of us could do a wheelie for ten feet. I looked at my Coke, then at Preech. "You can have half of mine, amigo."

Preech nodded his thanks and a grin slid across his lips as he watched Rudy ride off. "Methinks I'll loosen the lug nuts on that twerp's front tire. The next wheelie he does will prove exactly how far he can go."

CHAPTER 4

I poked my head through the gate and looked around. "So far, so good. Looks like the coast is clear in the backyard. Hey, if Mom grounds me 'til I'm eighteen, will you and Rudy at least mail me pictures of fish y'all catch?"

"I'll do you one better. I'll invent a time-bending machine, then we can freeze any day we want. We can fish for hours if we feel like it, and nobody but us will know."

I took a deep breath and wondered what kind of punishment was about to get heaped on me. "Thanks, man."

We walked our bikes to the side of the house then tiptoed to the back door.

I eased it open, and quietly closed the door behind us. Everything seemed normal, even Milly lying on the cat yelling, "Why you growl at me? I love you!"

The house smelled delicious, and I realized I had forgotten to eat breakfast. My stomach growled at me, reminding me it was way past lunch.

"Flowers, we forgot the flowers," hissed Preech as he grabbed my elbow.

We turned around and started for the back door and almost jumped out of our skin when Mom's voice boomed all around us. "Well, well, well, what do we have here? I just got off the phone with your other partner in crime. And his mom."

I turned and cringed to half my size. "Hello, favorite mother. How may we be of assistance to you this fine day?"

"Well, for starters, you can both apologize and promise to never do that again. I almost had a heart attack."

"Sorry," Preech and I said at the same time.

I noticed a smudge of flour on her forehead. "Looks like you've been workin' hard on something in the kitchen. It smells beautiful."

"Yes, I have. There are two dozen of my award-winning cookies cooling off on the counter. They will be excellent, and everyone but you two may have some."

I'd seen that steely gaze before. I knew from other times I'd taken a walk on the wild side it'd be a while before she thawed out.

"I am very hopeful you will work on more civilized means of getting permission to go fishing in the future."

"Yes, ma'am. It was a mob thing and I apologize for my lack of presence of mind," answered Preech. "I am sure we can figure out a better way to request permission in the future, and hopefully we will straighten up and fly right from now on."

Mom had told me to straighten up and fly right about a thousand times, and I noticed her lips go from flat to a bit of a smile. Preech was a genius.

I bent over all hunchbacked and rubbed my hands together and drooled a little.

"What jobs may we be lucky enough to do for you today, dear, sweet mother?" Normally that routine got a giggle and a pat on the head, but that time it didn't help at all.

She blinked a couple of times and said, "Today your tasks will be cleaning the bird cage, taking out the trash, vacuuming the den, weeding the front flower beds, sweeping out the garage, and cleaning your room."

Rats. My chores had doubled. I wondered if telling her about the monster fish I was going to bring her and the flowers Preech forgot would help anything, but something told me it'd be best to keep my lips zipped.

She looked at my leg and the bandage, opened her mouth to say something, then shook her head and walked away.

Preech pulled my arm and we headed for the front door. "She didn't say anything about you being grounded, so let's get busy before she does."

I nodded and looked back to make sure we were in the clear. "Is today Monday, buddy?"

"Yep. That means tomorrow is Tuesday. Which means..."

"We go to The Oracle's," we grinned and said in unison.

Every Tuesday we got to help out on Preech's Uncle Oliver's farm. He drank beer, knew something about everything, and was possibly the coolest person walking the earth. We called him The Oracle, (which had been another one of Preech's words of the day), but never said it to his face. Even though it sounded respectable, we would never do anything to disrespect him.

Since he was also an army hero, and not only a man, he was "The Man" as far as I was concerned. There was no way in a million years I could become a man like Oliver.

Preech and I looked over the weed-infested flower bed, sighed, and got on our hands and knees and started ripping.

Preech looked under the bushes, and I figured he was looking out for snakes. "The Oracle always says when you have a bunch to do, do the things you don't like first, then end with the things you like so it's kinda like dessert."

I pulled some weeds and put them on my head like a crown. "Yep, he also says that weeds are plants they ain't figured out a use for yet. When they do, we'll be millionaires!"

Preech laughed and stuck a handful of weeds on his head. In a British accent he said, "Jeeves, after our dirt bath we would love to go see the ducks. Warm up the car like a good chap and bring it over straightaway."

I cracked up. "So when we're done with this I reckon we flip a penny to put the other jobs in order. Then we can end with the bird cage. At least that crazy parakeet trying to peck our hands off is more fun than everything else."

I yanked out a huge wad of weeds, then realized I had also pulled out one of mom's geraniums. I quickly dug a new hole and patted the flower back in. "How many pranks do you figure you and Rudy have pulled on each other?"

Preech tapped his chin and looked at the sky. "Hundreds, I reckon. It kinda feels like the Russians and Americans, one-uppin' each other with nuclear weapons. And boy, do I have some doozies I'm workin' on. He's quite the worthy adversary when it comes to pranks, which is how I know he ain't a dumb guy. It just seems like he gives up on school and stuff when Ted is around."

"I know. It's crazy. It's like Ted has gone off the deep end. I heard from a guy that works at the Burger Shack that he orders his drive-through orders at the window, then sits there and eats them like he's inside the restaurant. He stacked up fifteen cars behind him the other day and laughed and said he can't wait till he tops it with twenty."

Preech pulled two fists full of weeds and threw them over his shoulder. "Rudy told me that when they go to public restrooms, Ted takes the toilet paper out of all of the stalls and sneaks it out under his shirt. He says it's to save money, and to teach other people resourcefulness. I think it's just plain mean."

I whistled and shook my head. "Speakin' of mean, did you see the marks on Rudy's back when he took his shirt off while we were fishin'? Do you think Ted wakes him up by throwing lit cigarettes at him or somethin'?"

"I dunno, amigo. Maybe The Oracle is our only hope for help, like Obi-Wan Kenobi. We can ask him tomorrow to see if he knows anything we can do."

We finished weeding the front bed, then flipped a penny to decide in which order to do the rest of the chores. Thinking it would be better to divide and conquer, we played rock-paper-scissors to see who did what. I got take out the trash and clean my room, and Preech got sweep the garage and vacuum the den.

We got done at about the same time and met in the kitchen to tackle parakeet Pete's cage together. I'd fished with bait bigger than Pete, and it amazed me something so small and pretty could be so nasty.

There were two sandwiches, potato chips, and fresh glasses of Tang on the table. Mom probably wouldn't be talking to me for a while yet, but it was good to see things were getting better. Preech looked hopefully at the cookies on the counter, but since there weren't any on our plates I shook my head. No sense in rocking the boat when it was just starting to float again.

I heard the car leave earlier and figured Mom took Milly to get a new tutu or something.

After we ate, Preech and I went to the garage and put on the thickest gloves we could find. I wasn't too worried about the bird mess, but was more scared of the ferocious beast ripping the skin off of my hands. We grabbed a blanket to wrap around the cage, hoping it would make the bird think it was nighttime and calm down.

We stood on both sides of the cage, ready for battle. Pete's beady little eyes flared at us. If he could talk, I'm sure he would have said "Bring it on," or some other tough guy wisecrack.

"Why does your family dig this bird so much, Kev man?"

"I dunno. He lets Milly put him on her shoulder, and he sits on the table every morning like he's reading the paper with my dad.

Nobody believes how psycho he gets when they aren't around, and sometimes I think they like this little bag of feathers more than me."

"Well, let's get this over with. I'm dying to play your new Atari."

Normally I would put a gloved finger through the back of the cage, and the little monster would clamp on to it while I yanked the old newspaper out and threw new paper in. I eased the blanket over the cage and slowly opened the door. There was a sliver of blanket open by the cage door to see inside.

I pulled the gunky old newspaper out, and set it in the trash can. We didn't hear a peep out of Pete. "Works like a champ," I smiled.

Next I slid the new paper into place. Preech and I nodded and grinned. The small door was just an inch away from clamping shut, when a blur of green and blue fury exploded out of the cage. Pete had grown the heart of a lion and the ferocity of a pterodactyl.

He buzzed out of the cage, clamped his talons onto my nose, and pecked my forehead so hard I thought he'd poked my brain. Next, Preech tried to get his hands up to protect himself but wasn't quick enough. Pete jumped on Preech's head, and hammered him so fast and so many times my eyes couldn't keep up.

Pete got a beak full of Preech's hair, and ripped it right out of his head. Preech screamed and dove under the table. I climbed under as well, wishing I had a gun or a bottle of holy water to fight the beast. Pete shot across the kitchen and landed in the middle of the cookies. He slowly looked back and forth from the cookies to me.

"No," I shouted from under the table. "Back in the cage."

Like he heard me and just didn't care, Pete kicked the cookies with his razor-sharp claws and batted them with his wings. Cookies flew from the plate like lopsided Frisbees.

"Five second rule," Preech shouted, as he scurried out from under the table to grab the cookies off of the floor. Preech froze when Pete stopped and cocked his head sideways at him, pure evil coursing out of his eyes. He crawled back under the table, and we hugged like little girls.

"Of course my mom and Milly are gone. He never does this stuff when they are here."

Preech winced as he rubbed the raw spot on his scalp. "What the heck do we do?"

Shattering glass echoed through the kitchen. Pete was walking down the counter, stopping only to nudge every one of mom's wine glasses until they fell over and exploded into a million pieces.

I cupped my hands around my mouth like a megaphone. "Bad bird. Stop that."

Then Pete hopped into the open flour jar, kicking and thrashing until a huge white cloud hung in the middle of the kitchen.

Preech grabbed the blanket and flung it over us just as Pete came screeching out of the haze. His wings were back like a dive bomber, and his eyes were locked on mine. The blanket had just gotten around us when I heard the thump of Pete against the fabric.

"Try not to speak, or breathe if you can help it," whispered Preech. "I think it's our scent and voices that make him go nuts."

We stayed under the blanket for what seemed like a week. The fear Mom would come back and see her kitchen destroyed was starting to tie my stomach up in knots. There was no way I could explain this, especially if I told the truth.

Preech slid next to me, putting his lips almost on my ear. "I've got it. Let's jump out at the same time and throw the blanket over the critter. Then maybe we can make a tunnel with it and force him back in the cage."

"Sounds like a plan," I whispered back. "Let's go on three."

On the count of three, we jumped out from under the table, using the blanket in front of us like a shield. We looked every direction at once, trying to find the psycho bird before he found us.

There were marks Pete made with the flour on the walls, counters, and floor, but no sign of him. Preech pointed to the knobs on the stove. The flour prints showed Pete had hopped on every one, like he had tried to turn the gas on and blow me and Preech to smithereens.

Preech arched his eyebrows and poked his chin towards the other side of the kitchen. "Aww man, you just can't catch a break today. Sorry, buddy."

CHAPTER 5

The window was wide-open. Nothing but a bright green feather rested on the windowsill.

I ran to it and poked my head out. Staring as hard as I could, I tried to find Pete flying around or hanging out in the trees. There were other birds and a lazy old alley cat licking its tail, but no Pete. I looked down and noticed two small flour streaks on the windowsill, making a sign that looked like an arrow. I thought Pete scratched the sign with his claws, laughing some maniac parakeet laugh before he flew to freedom.

Pete's last words probably were, "I went this way, sucker. And if you ever get done with being grounded, I'll be waiting to kill you when you leave the house. Sweet dreams," or something like that.

Preech eased his head out the window beside mine, squinting at the trees and sky. "That was the craziest thing that ever happened to me. He was like a whirling dervish of pain."

I started to laugh, but it caught in my throat when I looked back and surveyed the damage. "Well, we can vacuum the cookies clean and put them back on the plate, and clean up all the flour I guess. What should we do about Mom's wine glasses? She always cleans them before she has a bridge game, which is prob'ly today or tomorrow."

Preech scratched his head and looked at the piles of glass. "Do you reckon we have time to glue them back together?"

"I doubt it. On top of getting this all back to normal, we gotta figure out a way to get another bird that looks like Pete back in the cage before anyone gets home. I don't think there's another one as crazy as Pete on the planet. But, since they all pretty much look the same, we can buy a new one and stick him in the cage and no one will ever know. Right?"

Preech snapped his fingers. "Hey, how 'bout you put the bandage from your leg on the windowsill? Maybe the scent of your blood will bring him back and we can net him with the blanket. In the meantime, I'll run home and get some of my mom's wine glasses while you clean up."

"Deal. I'll give Rudy a call to see if he's close to bein' done. If he is, he can run by the pet store and get a new bird and come help clean up."

Preech gave two thumbs up and ran out the back door. I watched him yank all of the stuff off his bike and chunk it by the fence before he took off, to make him faster I guessed. What a good buddy.

I called Rudy's house, and his mom said it would be quite a while before he got done. She told me Rudy would call when he could come over, but I figured there was no way he'd be done in time to help.

It took a whole roll of wet paper towels to clean the flour off of the counters, and I almost cut my hand off scraping the glass shards into the trash. I pretty much ran out of every cuss word I knew as I thought about that bird.

I heard a screech of bike tires on the driveway, and smiled when I saw Preech with a bulging backpack slung over his shoulder. He carefully handed me the backpack through the open window, then stepped over the blood-stained pile of bandages on the windowsill and into the kitchen.

He was sweating and out of breath. "I saw Milly and your mom coming out of the grocery store, and took the alley short cut the rest of the way here. If they don't have anywhere else to go, I figure the best we got is five minutes. How's it goin'?"

I started to remove the wine glasses from their newspaper cocoons, trying to remember how the other ones were set up on the counter. "Well, I got everything cleaned up best I could, but no sign of the feathered fury. Rudy is still doin' stuff at his house, so unless a miracle happens we gotta come up with a good story about Pete."

Preech wadded up the newspaper pages and threw them in the trash. "Well, there's always the truth...it worked out pretty good with your dad's pit."

"I know, I know, but it feels like if I tell the truth that little psycho bird wins somehow. There's no way Mom'll believe me anyway."

"Yep, but maybe if I back it up she'll believe you and we can hunt him down and make things right."

I heard Mom's car pull up, then Milly's unmistakable whistling as she threw the front door open.

Preech got the last of the newspaper in the trash, then slipped his empty backpack and the blanket in the garage. I did a quick re-arrange on the wine glasses.

Mom walked into the kitchen, and set an armload of grocery bags on the table. She smiled as she slid her sunglasses back on her head, looking around the kitchen.

"Well, I am impressed. Not only did you get everything done, you went above and beyond by scrubbing the kitchen clean. Looks like two young men learned a very important lesson today."

I grinned and patted Preech on the back. "All his idea, my good lady. He thought it would be the right thing to do. We did hit a slight snag, though."

Her smile dropped to a frown. "A slight snag?"

I linked my hands together like I was saying a prayer. "Yes, we tried to work as fast as possible to surprise you, and I accidentally knocked your wineglasses over. But we borrowed some from Preech's mom, and I'll be more than happy to pay for new ones. Once I pay for dad's new barbeque pit, that is."

She looked around the kitchen again, then back at me. "Well, I guess accidents do happen. As a matter of fact, I got some new ones for Christmas that I stuck up in the attic. I've been meaning to switch them, so we can give those back to Preech's mom after my bridge game. Then I can start using the new ones."

Relief surged through me as one of the knots in my stomach came undone. "Oh, great. Very cool." Things were going so well, I wondered if I should say anything about Pete. A voice in my head screamed that it was gonna come out sooner or later, so I needed to just let it rip.

She gave me a hug, and rubbed Preech's head. "You know, I think you two may have earned some cookies for turning the corner like you did. How many would you like?"

I looked at the plate. Even though each cookie spent over a minute under the vacuum hose attachment, it seemed like they were still crawling with feathers.

Preech looked like he was thinking the same thing. "You know, that is super nice, but to really learn our lesson it may be best we don't. Thanks so much, though."

Mom shrugged and went to unpack the groceries.

"Well, Mom...there's one other thing."

She was reaching to put some cans on the top shelf of the pantry. "Yes, what's that?"

"It's like, umm, well it's about..."

Just then Milly walked in and screeched "Pete!" It was so loud I bet it made people in China jump a foot in the air.

Thinking she had seen the cage and was trying to get me busted (something she loved to do), I twirled to look at her. She was pointing to the cage, and my jaw almost hit the floor when I looked at it. There was Pete, in all five inches of his feathered glory, sitting on top of his cage. The last place in the universe I would have looked for him.

Preech saw Pete, then whimpered and backed up against the wall.

Milly walked over to the devil bird, and he chirped and jumped on her finger. She took it across the kitchen to Preech. "What's wrong with you, Mister Scaredy Pants? It's just a teenie-tiny sweet little bird. Don't you wanna give 'em a kiss?"

She thrust Pete at Preech's face.

Preech's eye started twitching like a butterfly in a tornado. "No, thanks, I think I'm a little allergic or something. Put him back. Please."

Milly kissed Pete on the head, then spun on her toes and skipped back to the cage. She opened the cage door, and Pete hopped in and started pecking at his food. No ripping Milly's hair out, no crazy dive bombs, just a regular-looking bird wanting to go home.

Mom let out a disgusted grunt and pointed to the window. "How gross. What is that?"

I walked to the window and grabbed the clean edge of the bandages. "Umm, that's what I was trying to tell you about. We were trying to see if blood turns brown if left in the open air." I slipped them into the trashcan.

"Well, boys, that is just nasty. We get enough flies in here anyway, so please conduct your experiments outside. Way away from the house. Okay?"

Preech grabbed my elbow and we walked out of the kitchen. "Yes ma'am, will do."

He whispered as we crossed the den, "I almost peed my pants when I saw the demon bird. How'd he do that?"

"I dunno. I think he left the feather on the window to throw us off, then prob'ly cruised around the house to try and find poison or something to take us out. We aren't dealing with your average birdbrain, my man. I may come sleep at your house for a while."

Preech shuddered. "No problem. I don't think I'm gonna be able to sleep for a week."

I smiled. "Maybe we can borrow a welder from The Oracle to weld the cage door shut. If we lock him in there for good, we may save the entire planet."

We turned on the TV and my Atari game, and plugged in Pong. Both of our mouths hung open as we watched the square ball dance back and forth across the screen.

"This is the best ever, Preech my man. There is no way they can ever make a game better than this."

"I concur," he said. I figured that was another word for "yep," but was too busy concentrating to ask.

We played ten straight games, and each of us won five.

The eleventh game started, and everything was on the line for the all-time world record Pong championship.

Rudy walked in, and definitely did not look like a happy camper. "What's up fellas?"

In the split second I turned my head to say hello, Preech slipped the winning shot past my little goalkeeper thingie.

Preech slapped me on the back, and looked at Rudy. "Hello meathead, would you like me to spank you at Pong first, or do you wanna save some time and just cry yourself silly on the floor now?"

Rudy shook his head. "Well, to be honest, I'd like to figure out a way to make a big galoot named Ted cry. He's back in town, and man is he on a tear."

I was so glad he was finally talking about Ted that I totally forgot I had just lost the Pong championship. "What do you mean?"

Rudy frowned. "Well, it's a real good thing we got everything done. He was way early coming back off the rig, and woulda gone berserk if everything wasn't perfect."

I wanted to ask what happened, but it felt weird because I just didn't want to know if Ted did something bad to Rudy.

"What do you mean he is on a tear?" asked Preech.

"Well, my mom said we should go do something together, so he took me to Jerry's to get some ice cream. On the way there, he honked at everyone that took a split second too long at a stop light or stop sign. Then, when we walked into Jerry's, he saw a kind of big lady sitting at a table by herself. He went up to her and asked when she was having her baby, but I think he knew she was just kinda fat all over but not pregnant."

Preech started to laugh, then frowned and shook his head.

I shook my head too. "Whoa, what did she do?"

"She started cryin' and ran out of the store with half of her ice cream still in the bowl. Then Ted laughed and said that maybe that'll make her get off her butt and get in shape."

Preech looked at the floor and sighed. "That just ain't right."

Then Rudy pinched the bridge of his nose and closed his eyes. "And the worst part is we were walkin' out and there was a different lady standin' by the corner. He told me to wait in the truck and went to talk to her. Then he came back to the truck said part of becomin' a man was figurin' things out, so I should figure out a way to get home. The other lady got in his truck, and he left me in the parking lot at Jerry's."

I agreed that part of being a man was figuring things out but couldn't understand why a man as big and strong as Ted would hurt women and kids half his size. Before I could stop myself, the words flew out of my mouth. "Has he ever, umm, hurt you or your mom?"

Rudy put his hands up like he was surrendering, and started to say something then stopped. After he stared at the carpet a while he said, "I just don't want to talk about it anymore, okay?"

I nodded and gave him the controller to play Pong.

He stared at the screen and blinked. "Well, we gonna play or not?"

Preech jumped up and restarted the game. "Maybe we can ask The Oracle for help tomorrow. He knows just about everything."

Rudy nodded his head. "Why not...if somethin' doesn't happen soon, I'm gonna snap. I got a plan, but I hope we figure another way before I have to pull the trigger."

CHAPTER 6

We rode our bikes with grins so big it looked like we were cruising to Disneyland. None of us had ever been there, but we couldn't imagine it being any better than The Oracle's place. Even though sometimes we did hard, hot, back-breaking jobs, it never felt like work. For two dollars an hour, all the Coke we could drink, and hanging out with one of the coolest people on the planet, we thought we should have been paying him.

Rudy lagged behind, then snuck up on Preech to rub his front tire on Preech's back tire. Preech yelped and went into a wobble that almost made him wipe out. "Cut it out, knucklehead. You'll pay for that one."

Rudy laughed and rode past Preech, making a wide circle to not get tangled up in the stuff that stuck out from Preech's bike. "Speaking of payback, somebody mailed me quite the nasty picture the other day. Would you have any idea about such a thing, twerp?"

A grin slid across Preech's face. "I have no idea what you are talking about. Was it a close-up picture of you or something?"

"No, it was a close up picture of Rosalynn...with something of mine hanging out of her mouth."

I knew exactly what he was talking about. A few Saturdays ago we'd camped at the Oracle's farm, and when Rudy was off squirrel hunting with his slingshot, Preech told me to cover him as he went into Rudy's tent. He came out with Rudy's toothbrush, then grabbed his mom's Polaroid and ran to Rosalynn's pen. Rosalynn was The Oracle's huge old hog, who spent pretty much every second just lying in the mud.

He put the toothbrush in her mouth, then took a picture. He hid the picture and slipped the toothbrush back into Rudy's tent. I was wondering when that was going to pop up.

Preech laughed and sped ahead. "I feel sorry for poor Rosalynn. It must have tasted awful."

We took off after him, and turned off the highway onto the crushed seashell road that led to Oliver's.

Preech slammed on his brakes and put his hand up for us to stop. Then he eased his kickstand down, slid off his bike, and started picking through his stuff until he found his slingshot. "It's a big one," he whispered, "could be a four-footer."

The Oracle paid us a quarter for every scorpion we killed, and a dollar for every rattle on a dead rattlesnake. When it came to snakes and dangerous insects, The Oracle was a "kill 'em all and let God sort 'em out" kind of guy.

Preech pointed under some bushes, and I squinted to see what he was talking about.

He put a shiny round ball bearing in the pouch on the slingshot, and pulled back with all of his might.

Rudy's laughter pierced the silence, making me and Preech jump. "It's a twisted stick, numbskull. Maybe you need glasses and a brain transplant."

Preech squinted hard at the stick, then shook his head and looked at Rudy. "At least I have a brain, squidhead."

He aimed his slingshot at the stick, and nailed the tip of it which would have been a perfect kill shot on a snake's head.

I smiled and patted him on the back. "You are the best dead-eye in the county, amigo. I bet you could shoot the antennas off a fly from fifty feet."

Rudy laughed again. "Maybe he could, if his smell doesn't melt the poor critter first."

A noise in the bushes across the road froze us in our tracks. It was getting louder, and coming right at us.

Preech thrust his hand back into his bag and almost dropped the new ball bearing before getting it in the pouch.

The Oracle's dog, Curiosity, sprang out of the brush, his tail wagging like a plane propeller. He jumped on Preech, licked his face, then did the same to me.

Preech wiped the slobber off on his shirt. "That's gotta be the happiest dog on the planet. I know The Oracle named him Curiosity so he'd get a cat if he saw one, but I think he would only lick it to death."

Rudy smiled and clapped his hands to get Curiosity's attention. "The poor thing will probably have to lick a rock until his tongue falls off to get your taste out of his mouth." He leaned down to rub Curiosity on the fur between his ears. "Isn't that right, Curi boy?"

I snickered. "I wonder what The Oracle has against cats. It seems like they'd at least help out with some of the snakes and other things."

Preech put the ball bearing back in its sack, then crammed the slingshot in with other stuff. "I dunno. As far as I can figure, he loves most everything in life but cats. Oh, and animals that can bite you and kill you. But that's about it."

I watched Preech finish checking his stuff, amazed that it all somehow hung on. "I wonder if a cat like a bobcat or mountain lion had anything to do with him losing his leg. Do y'all know how that happened?"

Rudy yawned and stretched. "I figured it happened to him in the war, but it took me a long time to even realize he only had one leg."

Preech's eyes grew wide. "Me too. If it hadn't popped off that day we were workin' the cows, I don't think he'd have ever told us. I always just thought he had a bad limp or somethin'."

Curiosity ran about twenty yards down the road to The Oracle's, then stopped and looked back. He was dancing and barking, making sure we knew he would guide us to the farmhouse.

We climbed back onto our bikes, ready to get the day going. As we came around the last corner and could see the house, we heard Oliver's booming voice from the porch. He was wearing the same overalls he always wore, and drinking coffee out of a metal thermos. "Mornin', Troopers! Y'all ready to hammer down today?"

We all grinned and nodded, and gave him a loud "yes, sir," that made him smile. As we parked our bikes and climbed on the porch to shake his hand, the smell that always hung around him tickled my nose.

No matter if it was first thing in the morning, or after working twelve hours in the sun, he always smelled sort of like WD-40. I reminded myself to remember to look for some of that stuff in the cologne store at the mall and buy a gallon of it. After I paid for dad's new barbeque pit, of course.

Oliver pulled out his chalkboard, where he'd written our jobs for the day. His sky-blue eyes gleamed behind his Coke-bottle glasses. "Today, gentlemen, is a full work day. But, I do have some surprises for each one of y'all during the breaks."

We looked at the board, and in perfect handwriting there were jobs listed with thirty minute breaks between each one. There was "Clean the Shed" with a "Kevin Break" after it. Next was "Clear the Brush by the House" with a "Rudy Break" after it. Then there was "Work the Animals" with a "Preech Break" after that.

I smiled and asked what the breaks were about.

"Well, I've been listenin' to what each of y'all likes to do, and made some changes around here. Kevin, what do you see by the pond?"

I squinted towards the water and saw what looked like a pole sticking out of the ground. "Is that a small flagpole?"

He chuckled and shook his head. "Nope. But you can't ever have enough ways to fly Old Glory I reckon. It's a pole I set in concrete so you can put your fishin' rod in it and fish all day. I figure a world-class fisherman like you is gonna fish every second of every break you can, so why not the whole time you're here?"

I grinned so big my eyes almost pinched shut. "Man is that cool. Thank you, sir. I'll make sure I make it quick to reel the fish in and release them. I don't want to cut into workin' time too much between the breaks."

He laughed and patted me on the shoulder. "I ain't worried about that at all. Just keep workin' hard like you do and everything will be all right."

Next, he looked at Rudy and pointed towards the pasture. "So for you, I figured our next great quarterback needs to keep sharp. You see what's out there?"

Rudy looked where The Oracle was pointing and yelped in surprise. "Is that a football field?"

Oliver nodded and grinned towards the short grass with white lines painted on it. "Well, it's half of one at least. If you work as hard at football as you do here, you're gonna be deadly anywhere from fifty yards in."

Rudy reached to shake Oliver's hand, making sure to look him in the eye like he taught us to do. "Thank you. That is awesome. Is it okay if I bring other guys from the team out sometimes? When we're not workin', of course."

"Heck yea, anytime. Just clear it with your coach and their folks and come throw the pigskin whenever you want."

Preech started looking around, anxious to see if there was a surprise for him.

The Oracle waved Preech towards the front door. "You don't think I'd forget you, would I, O Brilliant One?"

Preech grinned and shook his head.

The Oracle leaned into his house, using his cane to prop the screen door open. He re-appeared with a stack of magazines.

Preech grabbed one and hugged it to his chest. "National Geographic...a whole pile of 'em!"

Rudy and I glanced at each other and did our best not to crack up. Only Preech would be as excited about magazines as we were about fishing and football.

Oliver looked at me and Rudy and shrugged. "Well, the way I figure it, Preech is gonna be a great senator, astronaut, or doctor someday. Readin' each one of those is like taking a class on somethin', so when he mentioned they gypped y'all at the school by rippin' some pages out, I thought I'd buy all of them I could."

Preech thumbed through one magazine, mesmerized by the pictures and words. "Yeah, Principal Mackenzie says there is sometimes 'inappropriate' material in them, so he has to modify the magazines before they get to the library. You got any idea what he's talkin' about Oliver?"

"Nope. I just told a lady friend of mine who used to be a librarian to see about me gettin' my hands on some that had all the pages in them. That sweetheart got me a subscription, and is reachin' out to all her library friends to get me every one ever printed. I gotta say I enjoy readin' 'em as well."

Preech carefully laid the magazine on top of the others. "What I'll do is compare these to the ones in the library and see what pages got torn out. Then we can get to the bottom of this once and for all."

"Well, if I can help solve one of life's great mysteries for y'all, I'll call it a good day. Ready to get to work?"

We grabbed the work gloves he had laid out for us and walked to the shed. It was as big as our garage, and had stuff stacked in neat piles all the way to the ceiling. Sweat poured out of us as we moved everything out into the sun so Oliver could figure what to keep and what to throw away. In the very back of the shed were some old tools, the last things we had to take out before sweeping the shed and repacking everything.

As I lifted a rake, I didn't notice it had snagged on something far up on a shelf. The next thing I knew, the rake had pulled that thing off the shelf and it clobbered me on the head.

Once the dust settled and I stopped seeing stars, I looked down to see what had hit me. My heart stopped for a few beats as I realized I was looking at something that was going to change my life forever.

CHAPTER 7

A bundle of net-like stuff with lead weights sewn into it surrounded my feet. I didn't know what it was, but all I knew was that it screamed "I'm gonna make fishing better for you."

I looked at Preech. "What time is it, amigo?"

He looked at his wristwatch. "Exactly 9:59. Hey, that's almost time for a break."

I grabbed the awesome net-thingy and ran to the front porch.

Oliver was sitting in a rocking chair, whittling a piece of wood and whistling along with the radio. "Hey, trooper. What you got there?"

I climbed the steps and stood in front of him. A fan on the table worked hard to push the hot air off the porch. It felt like he'd laid a hair dryer down and turned it on full blast.

"I dunno. Something tells me it has to do with fishin', I hope."

He pushed his glasses into place and smiled. "Oh, yeah. That's a cast net. Great for catchin' bait."

It felt like the sun shined a little brighter, and I think I heard an angel play his harp. "So it does have to do with fishin'?"

"Yep. You betcha. You throw that out, catch little fish, then hook 'em and use them to catch bigger fish. You ain't seen one of those before?"

"No, sir, never. Preech was workin' on some invention to catch small fish to use as bait, but he says it's still in some kind of trial phase."

He chuckled and pushed on his cane to help him out of his chair. "Well, it's about break time for you fellas, and I say we get this thing back into action. And, since you are the number one fisherman, I'd appreciate it if you took the net as a gift. Call it an early Christmas present."

I looked at him and my mouth just wouldn't work to thank him.

He glanced back towards the shed and shook his head as he saw Preech and Rudy coming towards us. They were obviously arguing about something. "Those two bicker like a couple that's been married fifty years, but they do seem to enjoy it, don't they?"

I shook my head as well. "Yep. Those two could argue about how to spell the word dog, but they stick up for each other every chance they can. I'm just glad they don't join forces as far as pranks go. It could wipe out the whole universe."

"I agree. I reckon we both help them from time to time, but let's make sure we keep it fair. Deal?"

"Deal," I said as I shook his hand and looked him in the eye.

Rudy was puffed up and smiling, and looked like he was winning the argument. "So, chicken legs, it is forever known that a leg of lamb is the perfect weapon. Once you kill a bad guy with it, you cook it and eat the evidence and all is good with the world."

Preech shrugged his shoulders as he bowed to Rudy. "You have a great point. That's pretty good."

Then his eyes opened wide, and I could almost see the light bulb turn on over his head like in a cartoon. "Unless, O smelly one, the entire weapon disappeared."

Rudy's smile vanished, and he got the "Aww, man," look on his face. "What are you talkin' about?"

Preech puffed out his chest and spread his arms like the guy in the top hat at a circus. "Well, forever and ever and then some, it shall be known that the perfect weapon for killing a bad guy is an icicle. Not only can you wash it off and eat it, you can leave it on the ground or throw it in a river. Once it evaporates the fingerprints will disappear. Unlike fingerprints on the pork chop bone you were so proud of a few seconds ago."

Rudy grimaced. "It was leg of lamb, but anyway, you win. Again. Dangit."

Oliver made his way down the steps and motioned toward the pond. "C'mon Troopers, the Kevin break has gone up a notch."

We followed him to the edge of the water, and I carefully unrolled the net and gave it to him.

"So, what we got here is a cast net. You boys sure you never seen one of these?"

Preech scratched his head. "In my dreams I kinda did, but the one I was workin' on would need a truck motor and five guys to make it work."

Rudy raised his hand. "It's for catching the ignoramus fish, right?"

Preech smiled and pulled Rudy's hand down. "Yes, the ignoramus fish, exactly right, you big bull."

Oliver slipped the part of the rope with a loop in it around his hand. "This here is the land line. You curl up the line in one hand, grab the top weight on the net with your other hand, and let 'er fly."

He chunked the net, and it made a perfect circle right before it hit the water and disappeared into the depths.

Oliver counted to three, then pulled the rope back in. "You gotta let it settle for a few seconds, then ease it back to you by pulling the land line back in. The weights on the net wrap around everything under it, and if you timed it right you got yourself some bait."

We watched in awe as the net came out of the water. At first all I saw was long strands of green algae, but then, bingo. Squirming in and around the algae were minnows, small perch, and a very angry crawfish. Each one was perfect-sized bait.

I got so excited my knees almost stopped working. "Oliver, sir, that is the coolest, most excellent present anyone has or ever will give me. I just don't feel right takin' it, though. I could work for free till I pay it off, or I'll pay for it after I buy a new barbeque pit for my dad."

"Oh, yeah, for the one you messed up. Do you still play with lighter fluid?"

"No sir, and I ain't gonna touch another bottle of that stuff for a million, billion years."

Oliver did one of his huge belly laughs, something that always made us grin like jack-o-lanterns. I bet people a mile away could hear it if the wind was blowing right.

Once he caught his breath, he stooped down to look me in the eye. "Well, if you've learned your lesson, I say we build him one instead. Heck, we can build one for each of your dads."

Preech smiled and high-fived me, but Rudy looked down and kicked a rock with his shoe.

"An old buddy of mine works at the bakery, and they go through vegetable oil like water. It comes in fifty-gallon drums and throw them away when they're done. He's let me take some before, and I cut 'em in half and welded iron legs on them to use as cattle feeders. We can cut the top part like a lid, then put some legs on the bottom to make 'em into barbeque pits."

Just like that Oliver solved two of the biggest problems I had. If finding bait and getting my dad a new pit were off my mind, I could focus on the important things. Like getting to the island to catch monster fish, helping Rudy fix his problem with Ted, and becoming a man.

The Oracle picked the net up and eased the fish back into the water, shaking it to get the algae out as well. I almost had a heart attack, then realized we could catch bait like that anytime with the super cool net.

"Well boys, I'll have to ask your parents if it's okay for y'all to use the tools to cut up the barrels and weld the legs onto them to make pits. And I'll supervise each step, of course. Also, I can't pay y'all for your time makin' the pits, but if you can scratch together hinges for the lid and a handle I can scare up the rest around here."

Preech saluted him and grinned. "If I may, sir, can we make it that you just ask our moms? Since the idea is that they'll be presents for our dads and all."

"Excellent point. I'll make that adjustment and just ask the moms to get clearance. Speakin' of moms, guess what I had a discussion about with your mother, Corporal Rudy?"

Rudy cleared his throat. "Was it the bad decision we made about gettin' permission to go fishin' at Kevin's house yesterday, sir?"

Oliver shook his head and grinned. "Nope, but I'm sure I'd get a kick out of whatever that was. It was about chewin' tobacco."

Rudy's cheeks turned red. "You told her I asked you to try some?"

"Yep, I told her you've asked about thirty times, and I said my answer was always no."

Rudy sighed. "Well, I guess a thirty-first time ain't worth askin', is it?"

"Nope, as a matter of fact we talked long and hard about it. She asked me what I'd think would happen, and I said you'd prob'ly turn so green a cow would eat you if you walked across the pasture. I also told her more than likely it wouldn't kill you."

Rudy's eyes lit up. "Did she say I could try some?"

Oliver pulled the packet of Levi Garrett out of his pocket and tossed it to Rudy. "Yep, supervised of course. And there's plenty more where that came from."

Rudy peeled the pouch open, and pulled a wad out with his fingers. "Just stick it in my mouth and chew?"

"Yep, that's what you do."

Rudy opened his mouth, and packed the greasy ball of black gunk between his teeth. He smiled at us and puffed out his chest.

Oliver watched him chew and spit a few times, then squinted at Rudy. "How you doin' soldier?"

Rudy gave him a thumbs up, but then got a weird look on his face.

Oliver motioned for him to turn sideways. "You may want to point that direction, just in case."

We all knew about throwing up. We went to see *Rocky*, ate raw eggs for breakfast the next day, then ran into my backyard and threw up at the same time. But this was different. Rudy turned as green like a leaf, then light green like a perch, then as white as the belly of a catfish.

Oliver asked if he wanted some more, and Rudy shook his head and threw up all over the grass. I grabbed the cast net and held it above my head, making sure it wouldn't get any of the nastiness on it.

Rudy staggered back a few steps, then sat down hard on the grass.

Oliver looked at me and Preech. "Why don't you two go grab him a glass of water? While you're at it, grab a bottle of ginger ale too."

Preech and I took off for the house. Even though the net smelled funky from the algae and fish, I hugged it to my chest like it was a baby.

By the time we got back, Oliver had helped Rudy into the shade under an oak tree.

Rudy had gone from white back to perch green, so I figured he was headin' in the right direction.

Preech grinned and handed Rudy the ginger ale. "Hello, tough guy, can I get you anything? A cigar? Week-old tuna sandwich in an ashtray? Some more chewin' tobacco?"

Rudy burped and covered his mouth with his fist, like he was trying to block anything else from coming up. "No, punk, none of that, thank you very little."

He looked at me, his voice making a croaking sound. "Hey Kev, how long did you say it would be before you messed with lighter fluid again?"

I thought for a second. "About a bazillion years, or never. Whichever one comes first."

Rudy closed his eyes as he laid his head against the tree. "That may be how long it takes before I can even smell that stuff again without throwing up."

Oliver smiled and clapped his hands together. "Well, I'm glad to hear that, and your mom will be too. You should be all right once everything stops spinning, and in the meantime we'll get some hooks wet before the break is over."

Preech and I ran back to the front porch to get the fishing poles. The Oracle always had them ready to go in a rod holder he had made out of deer antlers.

We grabbed the rods, and I was about to go inside to look for the lure box when I stopped and smiled so hard my cheekbones hurt. We had a cast net now, and I would never have to fish with a little piece of wood that sort of looked like a fish for the rest of my life. With the net we'd always be able catch real live bait to put on our hooks.

Once we got back to the pond, I handed the poles to Preech. Then I went to check on Rudy. He had gone from perch green to green with red splotches on his cheeks. I figured that was an excellent sign he was going to live. Rudy gave me a weak smile and a wink when he realized I was there.

His voice wasn't so much a croak, but more like he'd just sucked some helium out of a balloon. "Catch a big one, buddy. I'll be there in a few minutes."

I handed the cast net to Oliver, and he got it ready to do its magic again. "Well Troopers, I'll show you one more time. Then it's your turn to dial this thing in."

I was so focused on his every move that I didn't hear the tires crunching on the crushed seashell road leading to the house.

Oliver stopped in mid-sentence as he recognized the car. "Aww, man. It's old lady Fenton."

Preech groaned. Rudy groaned louder. I almost started crying.

I figured maybe she really was a witch. Only something that unholy would come to turn me into dust on what was becoming the best day of my life.

CHAPTER 8

Oliver laid the cast net on the ground. "Okay boys, I think she may be the only person alive who doesn't like y'all. And she ain't got no problem speakin' her mind about it. Work with the cast net some until the break is over, then scoot on back to work."

Preech held Oliver's elbow to help him down the grassy slope. "Is she like a, you know, a kind of a witch or somethin', sir?"

Oliver laughed and turned his voice to a whisper. "I figure it would take an old priest, a young priest, and a whole gallon of whiskey to fix her head, but I'm pretty sure she ain't a witch. She sure does make a mean lemon meringue pie, bless her pointed little beak nose."

Preech and I turned to watch Oliver work his way to Miss Fenton's car, hopefully to take her to the porch so she wouldn't come mess with us.

I picked up the cast net, and it felt good in my hands. Like it should have been there forever. "You know, it seems like just about everyone in town comes to see The Oracle for somethin' every now and then."

Preech nodded. "Yep, people bring sick animals, busted farm equipment, and all kinds of other stuff. But you know, I never seen him take a nickel for his help. Have you?"

I thought about it. "Nope. You're right. I think some people just come to get the time with him. Like it makes you a better person by just breathin' the same air he does. The cakes, pies and cookies the other ladies bring sure are great."

Preech nodded faster. "Oh man, yeah. It's like having twenty grandmothers. Just get your head patted, cheeks pinched, and then you're rollin' in the treats."

Miss Fenton's voice pierced the air. It was somewhere between fingernails on a chalkboard, and slicing your leg by walking up against an open cardboard box. "Hello, numero uno Oliver. So glad to see you, but sorry those foul-mouthed hooligans are here wasting your valuable time. What's wrong with the big one? Hopefully he ate something poisonous, and then there will be just two I have to dispose of."

We did what Oliver had taught us, giving her our best fake smiles and waving like we meant it. Rudy had made it back on his feet but was still wobbly, like he had just gotten off a hundred-day boat trip. He tried to wave but had to put his hands back on his knees to stay standing.

Oliver patted her back and eased her towards the house. Miss Fenton pointed to the pie in her hand, then uncurled her bony finger and waved a "no, no" finger in our direction. She could tell him all day long that we couldn't have any, but by the time the dust settled behind her car on the way out he'd have an equal piece cut for each of us.

I grabbed the land line and slid it over my hand. Then I rolled the slack in my left hand, grabbed the top part of the net with my fingers like Oliver did, and chunked it into the water. His net had made a perfect circle, like the top of a mushroom. Mine looked like a wad of spaghetti.

Preech stared at the ring in the water the net had made, then back at me. "Well buddy, maybe it knocked a fish out and it got hung up on the bottom of the net. Pull it in and let's see."

There was nothing in or under the net, not even a measly drop of algae. So I tried again. The next throw looked like a pile of mashed potatoes. The next throw looked like a clown wig, and the last one looked like the Blob. Even though we hadn't got bait yet, I knew we'd figure it out.

Preech looked at his watch. "It's time to get back to work."

I grabbed his wrist to double check. "Aww, man, that only felt like thirty seconds. Sorry I hogged the cast net. You can have a chance next time."

"No problemo, amigo. Maybe The Oracle will put on another show, and I can mentally record his every move. He is the master when it comes to workin' that thing."

We looked towards the house. Miss Fenton was sitting in the rocking chair facing Oliver. When she noticed us looking at them, she got up and sat next to him on the porch railing. Then, where he couldn't see, she leaned back and grinned an evil grin, showing all of her teeth like a skeleton. She shook her hand at each of us, like she was holding an invisible cue ball.

Preech and I snapped to attention and did our wave and painful smile. Through his teeth he asked, "Do you think she's tryin' to put a curse on us?"

Rudy appeared next to me, finally able to stand up straight. "The only curse she has is the backside of her pants. It looks like two raccoons fightin' in a potato sack."

I jumped and grabbed Rudy by the shoulders. "He's back, baby, he's back! You feelin' alright?"

"Sorta back to normal, but man that stuff is wicked. That's one thing I wish I'd never done."

Preech pointed to the thick brush on the side of Oliver's house. "There's our next job, fellas. I say we take a wide circle around to the very back, then start workin' our way to the front. Maybe she'll be gone by then."

I pulled Rudy's arm over my shoulders. "Ten-four, and never leave a man behind."

Preech pulled Rudy's other arm over his shoulders. "Maybe Miss Fenton could have left some of those clothes behind. Is it legal to wear a polka-dot shirt with striped pants?"

We all laughed and took the long way to The Oracle's backyard.

Oliver said we could only use hatchets and machetes to clean the briars and brush. Our parents wouldn't let us get close to chainsaws until he said it was okay, and last time we asked him, Oliver did one of his humongous belly laughs and walked away.

We had gotten halfway to the front of the house when Oliver called out. "All's clear boys. Finish up the side of the yard, and it's a quick lunch and a football break. That is, if you're up to it Rudy."

Rudy grinned and looked at Oliver. "Well, sir, I'm not quite a hundred percent yet. Can we maybe do the Preech break-thing first, then mine later?"

Oliver chuckled and pointed to me. "No problem. Corporal Kevin, do you mind runnin' to get the mail?"

I set my machete against a tree and saluted him. "Sir, yes sir."

He saluted me back and eased into his rocking chair. He always told us to hustle from one thing to the next, so I took off at full speed to the mailbox. Curi ran next to me and looked frustrated I couldn't go any faster.

I brought the mail back and handed it to him. "Here you are, sir."

"Thank you very much. I sure do enjoy havin' you boys around, but the brain factory starts back up in a few weeks, doesn't it?"

It was closer to four weeks, five days, and nineteen hours. I was dreading going back to school and wanted the summer to last forever. "That's about right. I sure do wish I could stop going to school and just spend every day helpin' out around here and doin' man style stuff."

The Oracle smiled and nodded. "You know, that would be great, but what if not goin' to school changed history? In a bad way?"

"What do you mean?"

"Well, I read once that durin' the Civil War, a Confederate group was in a major battle, and the commander wrote a note to get reinforcements. But, instead of writing 'The battle is on,' he accidentally wrote, 'The battle is one.' When the other commander got the message, he thought it meant, 'The battle is won,' so they didn't go help out. If that fella had been a better speller, it could have changed the entire war."

I whistled and shook my head. "Huh, so something pretty small can change great big things?"

"Yep. You betcha it can. That's why getting a good education and workin' hard is key. I've run hundreds of soldiers under me, and runnin' you three is the most fun I've ever had. I'm just hopin' I can teach y'all a good work ethic out here, then you can take it with you as you live your lives. I'm hopin' it makes you better students, and someday better husbands and fathers."

And maybe a better man, I thought to myself.

Preech and Rudy had finished clearing the brush on the side of the house and were walking up the porch steps.

Rudy let out a laugh. "Well, Preech has got the school stuff licked, but we don't have to worry much about him being a husband and stuff. The only way he'll get a girl is if he gets good with that cast net thingy."

Preech's eyebrows shot up. "Oh really, yak breath? Since I'm a hundred percent sure you're the one who safety-pinned those shrimp under my bed, I shall repay you with putting chewing tobacco in every pillow you sleep on, every car you ride in, every—"

Rudy swallowed hard and interrupted him. "Uncle, uncle. You win. You are very good looking, and should have no problem getting a wife someday. You're the man."

Preech grinned and nodded.

Oliver chuckled and started to go through his mail. He pulled one letter out and smiled. "I sent this old salty dog a letter a few weeks ago. We've known each other since we were knee-high to a grasshopper, and he figured he'd go in the navy while I went to the army."

He ripped the letter open, and after reading it, Oliver put it down and looked at us. His eyes sparkled like fireworks. "Well Troopers, what do you say we take a road trip and go lookin' for some real-live pirate treasure?"

CHAPTER 9

Preech rubbed his hands together and smiled at Oliver. "Did you say pirate treasure?"

"Yep, could be. My buddy Sam is retired like me, but he still runs around on the water in Florida with his navy pals. His letter said they had a tropical storm blow through there the other day, and while they were lookin' around at the damage, they accidentally hung an anchor on a wreck."

Rudy's eyes grew wide. "What pirate's ship was it? Did they already pick up all the gold and stuff?"

Oliver laughed and flipped the letter to me to take a look. "It didn't say pirate ship for sure, since it could just be an old shrimp boat or somethin'. But, nobody had seen it there before, and it's in only about fifteen feet of water so it's easy to get to. I had mentioned you three in my letter, and he'd like to meet y'all and show you the sights."

Preech jumped up and ran for his bike. I knew he was going to get his pad and pencil, something he always did when he got real excited about something. He loved to make checklists and draw up plans for things we might need. Rudy loved to sneak it every now and then to erase checkmarks and drive Preech crazy.

Oliver picked up his chalkboard and wiped it clean with the eraser. "Well fellas, I say our mission for today just changed. You gotta stay flexible to make sure the important stuff gets done."

Preech ran back up to the house and took the front steps two at a time. He had opened his notebook and his pencil was at the ready. "Well, sir, where do we start?"

Oliver scratched his chin and looked out over the pond. "Well, for starters I figure we need to ask your folks if they're okay with it. I'm thinkin' a good ol' fish fry would be the best way to get them out here, then I can show them the camper and other stuff to answer any questions they got."

Rudy looked at the small camper squatting on the side of the house. "You reckon we can all fit in there, sir?"

"Nope, that would be a mighty tight fit. I'll show them that we'll have the camper and cab of the truck to sleep in if the weather gets nasty. Otherwise, it'll be me and Curi in the camper and you three in the big army issue tent I got."

Preech's pencil flew across the page. "Okay, we need fishing stuff, food, matches, a cast net, beer for Oliver, and dog food for Curi and Rudy. Can you think of anything else?"

Oliver chuckled and looked at the notebook. "Nope, that hits most of the high points. Somethin' you boys may want to do is figure out a way to get down to the wreck. I got some old masks and fins that might work, but I bet you three could figure out a way to stay on the ocean floor to poke around some."

Preech beamed. "Like invent somethin'?"

"Yep. Let's say we take a lunch and work the animals, then we'll spend the rest of the day makin' you fellas into scuba divers."

Preech saluted him and pointed at the shed. "I think I saw some old water hoses and other stuff." He looked at Rudy. "C'mon, pack mule. I might need help carryin' it back."

Rudy bowed and motioned towards the shed. "Ladies first, shrimpenstein. Don't stop or I might step on you like a bug."

Oliver pushed himself up out of his chair. "Can I get your help with fixin' lunch?"

I stood and opened the door, tingling with the thrill of finding real pirate treasure. "This sure will be a fun trip."

Oliver patted me on the back as he walked in the house. "You betcha it will be. Do you reckon your folks will let y'all go?"

"I'm sure I can, as long as my chores are done, and I think Preech will be able to go since his family loves new adventures and stuff. And Rudy would walk there barefoot on broken glass to get away from Ted, so I hope his mom lets him go."

"You know, I'd only seen that Ted fella around a few times before they got married last Christmas. He moved here right before they got hitched, right?"

"Yessir, I think he moves around a lot with his oil field work. I don't wanna sound disrespectful, but I'm not thinkin' he's a good guy. From what Rudy says and all."

"You know, that's the word around town. Ted acts grumpy as a bull that's got his belly covered with ticks, and he shoots his mouth off a lot. It's a shame, since Rudy's mom seems like such a good lady."

"Well, she said he was a prince when she married him, but has turned into a frog. I'm worried Ted is doing more than just being a jerk to Rudy and his mom."

Oliver stared at me. "Do you reckon he's hurtin' them? Like smackin' them around?"

"I'm not sure. We've asked Rudy, but he won't talk about it."

"I've always been taught to not mess with another man's business, unless he crosses the line. Find out if he's doin' any of that junk, and we'll get the law involved. If we hear he's hurtin' Rudy or Daisy, he better hope the law gets involved before I do."

A wave of relief washed over me. A real army hero like Oliver could kill a man three times before he hit the ground. If Oliver helped us with the Ted problem, I thought finding pirate treasure and saltwater fishing might just beat out fishing the island...maybe.

I followed him in the kitchen, and he motioned for me to grab a box full of MRE's off the shelf. "Do you remember what MRE stands for?"

"Yessir, it's meals ready to eat, right?"

"You are correct, soldier. What kind would you like?"

"We all like the peanut butter. It's better than anything you can buy at the store."

"Well then, peanut butter it is. Why don't you get one out for each of y'all."

I dug through all of the cool army-green packages until I found peanut butter, crackers, and a pecan roll for each of us. "So this is what real army soldiers eat in the field?"

"Yep. I can't count how many I've eaten, and they are handy while you're out huntin' or on the tractor. Take all you want for you three, and I'll just scare me up something else. Then I'll fetch my road map and we'll get to plannin'."

I pulled the bottom of my shirt out like a sack and put all of the MRE's in it. As I backed out the screen door onto the porch, Preech saw me and met me at the bottom of the steps.

He was grinning and holding diving stuff. "Well, I found two masks, four flippers, some buckets, and about eight miles of old water hoses. Gorilla boy is going through the last few boxes in the shed to see if there is anything else that might work."

I handed him his rations. "Excellent. That stuff might be exactly what we need."

Just as Preech opened his peanut butter, it slipped out of his hand and fell to the dirt. He picked it up, and noticed the top layer was caked with dirt and small pebbles. "Aww man. Do you think I can get the top back on and give it to Rudy?"

I laughed. "That might be kinda tough."

"All right then, since The Oracle says we should never waste anything, I'll spread the contaminated layer across the big rock Rudy sits on to eat. Maybe it will bring in some ants, then they will bite him, and therefore it won't go to waste."

He scooped the top layer of peanut butter out with his fingers and wiped it on top of the rock.

Rudy came out of the shed with his arms full of wire. "Hey fellas, they say baling wire and bubble gum can fix anything, so here we go."

Preech nodded. "Yeah, it'll fix anything but you, Frankenstein. You hungry yet, or do me and Kev get to eat yours?"

Rudy dropped the wire by Preech's feet and grabbed his lunch. "I'm starvin'." As he sat on the rock, he slipped a little but didn't look down to see why.

Preech smiled and coughed, obviously hiding a laugh.

Oliver came out of the house and took a seat on a lawn chair he had set by the rocks under the tree. He was balancing a sandwich on top of his beer and had a map tucked under his arm. "Will you fellas grab the map and unfold it?"

Preech got the map, and we each took a corner and opened it up.

Oliver pushed his glasses up on his nose, then pointed to a spot on the map. "That's where we need to get, and I reckon if we double-time it and drive all night we should get there in a couple of days."

Preech whistled and stared at the map. "How cool is this! If you start in one place, you can get almost anywhere."

Rudy smiled and traced his fingers over the colored lines. "Looks like football plays to me. See, there's a post pattern, that one is a curl pattern, and the long ones are all streaks."

I scratched my head and tried to focus and make sense out of the crazy marks and squiggly lines. "It looks like the verigross veins on my Aunt Karen's legs."

Oliver started laughing so hard his beer almost slid off the armrest he had set it on. "Boy, I never know what I'm gonna hear outta you three. It will be great to have your help as copilots, since the truck pulling the camper is about as nimble as an aircraft carrier."

Preech saluted Oliver. "More than happy to enlist, sir. Sorry about Rudy though. He's about the ugliest stewardess you'll ever see, but he could come in handy with wraslin' gators or somethin'. Or gator bait, if we need it."

Oliver gave Rudy a thumbs up. "I'll take that into consideration. Once y'all are done eatin', police the area clean then get to the animals. I'll go in and call your folks to see when they can come out to dinner."

We stood and picked up all of the empty MRE containers and Coke cans.

Oliver got to the top of the stairs and looked back at us. "Preech, why don't you feed the chickens, Kevin take care of the donkey, and Rudy slop the hog."

We stood straight, saluted him, and gave him a loud "yes, sir!" Then we took off to knock out our duties as fast as possible.

I finished feeding and watering the donkey when I happened to look toward Rosalynn's pen. I thought I had seen everything, until I saw a pig turn into a cheetah.

CHAPTER 10

Maybe cheetah wasn't the right word, but before then I'd seen rocks move faster than Rosalynn. As Rudy leaned over to dump the slop bucket into her trough, she bolted across the pen. Just before she got to him, Rosalynn went airborne like a fat kangaroo and buried her snout right in his butt.

Rudy yelped as the momentum flipped him over the trough. He landed in a sitting position and skidded to the fence.

Preech walked up and was trying to tell me something but started laughing so hard he couldn't talk. All he could do was point at the backside of his pants, then at Rudy, then at the rocks where we had eaten.

After five or six times I realized what he was trying to say. "The peanut butter?" I whispered.

Preech nodded furiously as he held on to my shoulder to keep from falling down. "I will forever lose it when people say 'when pigs fly,'" he wheezed.

Oliver heard the commotion and limped out onto the porch. Rosalynn had knocked over the trough and was just about to take a bite out of Rudy when he scrambled over the fence.

"What in the world has gotten into you, crazy ole' pig?" Oliver hollered. "C'mere Rudy, let's take a look. Are you hurt?"

"No sir, don't think so. It just felt like getting blindsided by a linebacker is all." Rudy looked at Preech, and his eyes turned to slits. "Would you know anything about this, punk boy?"

Preech wiped the tears from his eyes. "What a horrible thing to say. I was crying because I was worried something might happen to you. They can't give the pea brain of the year award to anyone else in town."

"Uh-huh," muttered Rudy as he walked up the steps.

As Oliver inspected the back of Rudy's jeans, I noticed that either the hog slobber or dirt had wiped off the peanut butter.

"Why don't you go inside in the bathroom and use the mirror to look and see if she broke the skin. If so, we'd need to get something on it quick."

Rudy walked into the house, and Oliver looked out at Rosalynn. "I ain't never seen her act like that. We'd better keep an eye on her, and I'll do the feedin' from now on."

Preech walked over to the pen and stuck his hand through so Rosalynn could sniff it. "I think she's fine now. Kevin and I will take care of feedin' her since I think that she confused Rudy's nasty smell for her slop. The good news is now he's got a date for the school dance next year."

Oliver looked at Rudy as the screen door squeaked open. "Everything okay?"

"Yessir, no blood, just a big red mark." He put his hands on his hips and tapped his foot on the porch, looking towards Preech. I could tell he knew Preech had something to do with the Rosalynn attack and was sure he was planning his next move.

Oliver poked his cane towards the masks and fins. "Well boys, why don't you three get to work on the diving equipment, and I'll meet y'all at the pond in a few minutes."

As we walked to the water, Preech showed us a diagram he had drawn. "I think it would be best to use the balin' wire to secure the hoses to the masks, then our hands will be free to pick up the piles of gold doubloons and swords and stuff."

"Sounds like a plan. Now that I don't have to pay for my dad's pit or bait anymore, I'll be able to hire a servant at my house to do my chores and jobs for Mom. And maybe a lion tamer to clean Pete's cage."

Preech nodded and smiled. "I'll be able to buy every machine ever made so I can work on my projects, the first of which will be a bionic leg for The Oracle."

Rudy shrugged and stared at his feet. "I think I'll buy Ted a one-way ticket to the sun, but tell him it's a trip to go beat up baby seals or something so he'll get on the plane."

I wanted to tell him The Oracle was willing to help out with Ted but figured I'd wait until it was just the two of us.

Preech grabbed the end of a water hose and attached it to a mask with so much baling wire it looked like a crazy bird nest. "Okay, I'll test this one. Kev man, you just stick the other hose in your mouth and see if it works better."

We took off our shoes, put the masks on, and eased into the water. As we got chest deep, Preech pointed down in the water and we smiled at each other and dove to the bottom.

Then we bobbed right back up. Then we swam down again, and bobbed back up.

Preech took off his contraption so he could talk. "I remember something in a diving story I read that said divers need weighted belts. I reckon it's so it'll pull them to the bottom."

"What if we got some of the empty burlap sacks and filled them with dirt? There's about a hundred of them in the shed."

Preech clapped his hands. "Brilliant. We can put dirt or sand in them for weight, and tie the strings from the top of them to our jeans. That way we can still use our hands."

Rudy had been standing on the side of the pond, feeding the water hoses to us. He said, "I'm on it," and took off for the shed.

When he was out of earshot I turned to Preech. "Good news. The Oracle said he'd help take care of Ted if he's hurtin' Rudy or Daisy."

Preech blinked water out of his eyes. "Cool. What if Ted's not hurtin' them, but just being a nutcase?"

"I dunno. He said to find out if Ted was crossin' the line and let him know. He also said Ted better hope the law finds him before he does if Ted's up to no good."

"Man, I'd pay good money to watch him hammer Ted."

I saw Rudy running back with a couple of sacks. "Me too, amigo. Me too."

We filled the sacks half-way full of dirt, attached them to a belt loop on our jeans, and carried them with us back into the water. Once we got chest deep again, Preech gave the sign and we sank on the bottom. And stayed there.

I couldn't see anything in the murky water, but I could feel Preech and hear him blowing air bubbles just a few inches away. We stayed on the bottom sucking air from the hose into our mouths, then put our tongues in the hose while we blew the air out of our noses.

All of a sudden, I heard Preech scream and splash to the surface. I was sure a big catfish attacked, once it figured out it was us who'd been trying to get him.

I stood up and rubbed the water out of my eyes. The first thing I saw was Rudy, laying on his back howling and laughing. He was holding the end of Preech's hose, and his legs were pumping like he was riding an invisible bike.

Preech coughed and scraped his tongue with his fingernails. I noticed something on his lip, and peeled off a tiny black leg. I held it up and looked at Rudy, and couldn't stop a laugh when I said, "Grasshopper?"

Rudy pointed to the end of the hose in his hand. "No, it was a cricket. And it only took five minutes to make the trip!"

Preech grinned and shook his head. "Touche', dirtbag. I'd start sleeping with both eyes open if I were you."

Oliver came towards the water, a huge grin on his face. "Well Troopers, looks like there's gonna be a hoedown at casa de Oliver tonight. I talked to your folks and they are all right with the trip, so they're gonna come out to see what we've been up to."

We slogged our way out of the water, carrying the sacks that had somehow gotten ten times heavier.

"Did y'all figure anything out with the diving equipment?"

Preech smiled a sly grin. "Yessir, figured we needed weight to keep us on the bottom, so I hope you don't mind we borrowed some old sacks. I just think it's Rudy's turn, and I'll be happy to hold the hose for him."

"Well, if it's figured out then we'll need to get moving on the other stuff. Rudy, what say you come in and help me get the picnic tables and chairs together? Can I count on you two to get some fresh catfish for tonight?"

I stood at attention and saluted him. "Yes, sir. I'll put my best man on it."

"Good. You may want to try the other side of the pond, since all the commotion prob'ly spooked 'em on this side. I'll work the cast net, so go grab the bait bucket and the old shrimp in the freezer to use as well."

Preech and I untied the sacks, shook the water off best we could, and took off for the house.

On the way back, Preech was playing with the spring latch on the lid of the bait bucket. "So how do you figure live bait beats everything else?"

"Well, I'm always tryin' to think like a fish, so one day I started to think of what it would be like if they fished for us."

"What do you mean, like threw lines and hooks out for us to bite?"

"Yep, kind of. Just think if one day they threw a line out with a bag of chewin' tobacco hooked on it. What would happen?"

"Well, The Oracle might grab it, but we wouldn't mess with it. And Rudy would run like it was the plague."

"Exactly. That's what I think lures are like. There might be just one or two fish that look at it and say, 'Wow, that looks good. I think I'm gonna bite it.' But what would happen if the fish threw a peanut butter MRE, or a bottle of Coke out on a hook?"

"Well, we'd hop on it like chickens on Cheetos."

"Bingo, my man. Now that we're able to fish with what they love to eat, we will be unstoppable. And thinkin' about it is why I put the fish back in the water fast. I know if they caught me and I wasn't a keeper, I'd really like it if they threw me back on the land super quick."

We made it back to the pond and Oliver pointed to six small perch, eight minnows, and three crawfish flipping around in the grass. "Not bad for two throws. Get the bait in the bucket, and give me a holler if y'all need any more. We'll be at the house gettin' things ready."

Preech and I put some water in the bucket and stocked it with the bait. As we walked around the pond, Preech started laughing. "So if the fish tried to catch us, would it be called goin' humaning?"

I cracked up. "Yeah, I guess so. The dad fish would say, 'Honey, me and the boys are going humaning tomorrow. Warm up the mud to cook 'em in. And tell Junior summer's almost over, and like it or not, he's just going to have to leave the school."

We both snickered as we got to the other side. Preech reached into the bait bucket and pulled out a perch. "So do we just hook it in the back?"

"Only if we were after bass. Since we're tryin' to get catfish, I say we cut them into pieces for bait. Catfish smell things better than bass, and they'll find it quicker that way."

We had two poles in the water, and by the time we got bait on the other two, we had fish on. Within thirty minutes, there were eight keeper-sized catfish on a piece of rope we used as a stringer.

Oliver came down to the pond and inspected our catch. "Great job, fishermen. That should do it. Everyone will be here in a couple of hours, so let's get these cleaned and ready to cook."

We carried the fish and poles back to the house.

Oliver pointed to the cleaning table he had set up. "Get the water hose pulled over there to clean as you go, and make sure to keep the innards and skin."

Preech wrinkled his nose. "Are we gonna eat that too?"

Oliver chuckled. "Nope. An old Indian taught me to put that stuff in with seeds we're gonna plant in the garden. Y'all can mark the ones we plant with fish parts and see how much better they grow."

Preech gave Oliver two thumbs up. "We sure don't waste nothin' around here. I'll draw up a diagram that marks the plants that'll have the guts and stuff."

"Well, knock yourself out, soldier. If y'all's folks let me teach you how to be safe marksmen, maybe they'll let you deer hunt with me this year. When we get one, I'll show y'all how to use everything but the earwax."

Preech tapped his head. "Great. Maybe we can do a brain transplant on Rudy, but we'd have to get the concrete out of there first."

Oliver laughed and nodded. "Well, okay then, we'll get right on that. When y'all are done cleanin' the fish, go cut some straight branches. I want to make back scratchers with the arrowheads y'all found by the creek as a gift for everyone to take home with them."

"Yessir," we said in unison.

Later our families arrived, and Oliver showed them around. He laughed, joked, and told everyone about how hard we worked and what a good job we did for him.

Little did we know that in just a few days, he would be fighting for his life.

CHAPTER 11

It was the day before the trip and about ten thousand degrees in Preech's garage. Rudy wiped the sweat off his forehead, but it immediately reappeared. "Dude, I'm about to melt. What all do we need to get?"

Preech pulled the sheet of paper out of his pocket. Sweat dripped off of his nose, smearing the ink marks on the page. "I figure we get four inner tubes, and the best design is to tie them together like a four-leaf clover. Then we can set plywood on top and tie a lawn chair to it. The Oracle can sit in the chair and fish with us while we wade fish."

"Ohh, real smart Gilligan. And what will happen when a wave comes and smashes the poor guy into a reef or something? And can he swim with just one leg?"

Preech yanked an inner tube from behind a pile of camping stuff. "No, ding dong, he won't use it in the surf, he'll use it in the bays. I read that the water is a lot calmer, and he said we're gonna fish both the surf and the bays. We'll cut a long piece of cane he can use as a push pole."

I stood between them to break it up. "Guys I think it's a great idea, and he's really gonna like it. How 'bout we get what we need and carry it to his house to build it. Then The Oracle can tell us exactly how he wants it done."

Rudy and Preech nodded their agreement, and we found the inner tubes, rope, and a piece of plywood.

As we dragged it out of the garage and laid it next to our bikes, Preech looked at the pile and scratched his head. "Well donkey boy, you're gonna earn your keep today. If you carry the plywood, Kev and I will get the tubes. Then I'll give you a pump on my bike to get back."

Rudy picked up the plywood and balanced it on his head. "I think I'll let Kev give me a pump. There's no way your rolling gizmo heap can carry anything else."

Preech and I each fit the tubes around our stomach and neck and climbed on our bikes. He looked like a Pixy Stix with two Life Savers attached to it, and I felt like a sumo wrestler.

As we turned onto The Oracle's property, Curi ran towards us and met us with a growl. Once he finally recognized us, he wagged his tail and danced just inches from our front bike tires. For once I wasn't worried about wiping out. Since I had the inner tubes on, I'd probably just bounce and roll up to The Oracle's front door.

Oliver had a huge pile of stuff next to the truck and smiled when he saw us. "We ain't leavin' till tomorrow. You boys must be as excited as I am to get here this early."

Preech slid his kickstand down and was getting off his bike when an inner tube hung on some of the stuff attached to his bike. He pulled everything down on himself, and Rudy laughed so hard he dropped the plywood.

Oliver bent to give Rudy a hand. "What you got them tubes for?"

Preech smiled and pulled the diagram out of his pocket. "For you, sir. We figured we'd make you a floating chair-thingy to fish from in the bays. Since you said the other day it felt like you'd be glued to the sand while we wade fished in Florida."

"Well, ain't that the nicest thing. I appreciate it, boys. Maybe we got time to test it on the pond here before we pack it, just to make sure."

Rudy pulled a small ice chest out of the wreckage that was Preech's bike. "And, we pooled our cash to get you this. You can pack it with beers when you fish with us."

The Oracle smiled so big you could see his top and bottom teeth. "Well, I always say 'To think like a fish you gotta drink like a fish. Thank you, Troopers." Let's give this contraption a whirl."

We carried everything to the pond and put it together. Oliver used the cane push pole to help get on the vessel, and smiled and nodded when he sat in the chair. "This'll work fine. Thanks again."

He pushed himself all around the pond, and I loved seeing him grin like a little kid.

As Oliver pushed his way back onto the bank, he saluted us and held the push pole up in victory. I noticed the scars and marks on his fingers and knuckles. You couldn't put a quarter down on his hand without hitting one, and I wondered how many were from workin' the farm and how many were from fighting bad guys in the war.

I looked at my hands, and there were hardly any on mine. I wondered if I'd have to get in a lot of fights or have to have my hands mashed by machines and animals to finally become a man.

"Why don't y'all get this disassembled and bring it up to the truck. I'll start loadin' the other stuff, and we'll just rope your invention on if we need to." Oliver walked towards the house, whistling and using the push pole as a cane.

As we started to untie the ropes that held the tubes and plywood together, Curi brought a tennis ball and dropped it at my feet. He was always ready to play fetch, and loved it when we threw the ball in the water for him to go get and bring back to us.

Rudy chunked it in the water and Curi took off after it. "Do y'all remember that super cool neighbor of mine, Miss Greenbaum?"

Preech nodded as he worked on a knot in the rope. "Yeah man, she's awesome. She's the one that gives out two big candy bars at Halloween, right?"

"Yep, that's her. She also comes to my house the day after Halloween." He used his best lady voice and said, "'Rudy dear, please save me from myself and take these. A minute on the lips, forever on the hips,' then she gives me any extras."

"I know where I'm going the day after Halloween this year," Preech said as he started on the last knot.

"Well, I was in the backyard and heard Ted talking to her. He was saying things like 'You can't tell anyone, or they'll think you're going crazy and might take your license away.'"

The hair on the back of my neck sprung up when I heard Ted's name. "What was he talkin' about?"

"I couldn't hear everything, but I saw her give him twenty bucks. And he kept saying to keep quiet and everything will be okay."

Preech got the last knot undone and started to gather the rope into a loop. "Why'd she give him twenty bucks?"

"After Ted took off, I snuck in her garage to look around. She's got a tennis ball hangin' on a piece of string attached to the ceiling. When it touches her windshield, she knows to stop her car."

Preech stopped coiling the rope. "And Ted stole the tennis ball?"

"No, worse. I saw an extra nail hole in the ceiling, a couple of feet from where the tennis ball's attached. I think he snuck in there and moved the ball so she'd keep going and smash her car into the wall. After that he swooped in like Mr. Nice Guy to fix it and get paid."

Preech shook his head. "Man, that's dirty pool. And that's why he told her to zip it, so she wouldn't tell anyone who might come in and figure it out. And he prob'ly moved the tennis ball back when he was fixin' the wall."

"Yep. He's like a nightmare that keeps getting' worse."

I couldn't stop the words from flying out of my mouth. "I talked to The Oracle about Ted, and he's willin' to do whatever he can."

Rudy looked at me and blinked, then gave me a small grin. "Well, thanks guys, but my mom said she's gonna talk to him about getting some kind of help or something. Like from a doctor, if he'll go to one."

Preech grunted. "Well, I wish we could just go talk to him, but the dude's so big it's scary. I think he'd pick me up and throw me like a dart if he wanted to."

Rudy smiled and slapped him on the shoulder. "If the doctor doesn't work, maybe your freakishly big brain can figure somethin' out."

"I'm on it. Let's get this stuff to The Oracle. I gotta get home and pack up."

We gathered the inner tubes and plywood and marched it all to Oliver's truck. He had separated everything into piles and whistled as he picked through them. "Alright, looks like we're gonna have to put the lighter stuff in the camper, and the rest we can rope in the back of the truck.

"Sir, should I bring the cast net? Will the salt water hurt it?"

"I was countin' on you bringin' it. They work great in salt water. I was also pleased when I saw that you washed it off and dried it after we used it the other day. You take care of your tools, and your tools will take care of you."

Preech set the tubes and plywood in the back of the truck. "Well, sir, I've gotta get home to get my stuff together. You need help with anything else?"

"Nope, I've got it handled. We're shipping out at Oh Five Hundred, so we'll see you then."

I gave Rudy a pump on my bike back to Preech's, then went home to pack.

During dinner, my trip was all we talked about.

Milly bent over like a bird to eat her spaghetti, sucking each noodle in like a worm. Between bites she machine-gunned me with questions. "So, you gonna bring me back pretty seashells? What happens if you catch a mermaid? What if the pirates catch you stealin' their gold, and they feed you to the crabs? Why ain't I goin'?"

My mom told Milly to go to the kitchen to get more bread. I thought it was so we could get a word in edge-wise. "That is very exciting. What are you looking forward to most?"

"The treasure is huge, but Oliver says his friend will show us great fishing spots and other cool stuff. Thanks for letting me go."

My dad reached over and rubbed my head. "You got it, sport. We'll miss you, but it should be quite the adventure."

After helping with the dishes, I went through my fishing stuff and the clothes Mom had packed. There were four pairs of underwear, and since we were going for three days and would be surrounded by water I unpacked two of them. That made room for six more bags of hooks.

It felt like my head had just hit the pillow when I heard my dad's voice. "Time to go, buddy. Wouldn't want you to miss the bus."

I looked at my alarm clock, and it said four o'clock. My eyes flew open, and I thought that if school was at the beach I'd never have trouble getting up.

We got to The Oracle's and saw Preech standing on top of a huge heap of stuff in the back of the truck. His dad was laughing with Oliver as they tied ropes around everything. Rudy's mom pulled up a few minutes later and dropped him and his stuff off.

Oliver smiled and said, "The posse's ready to roll."

Rudy looked in the cab of the truck, then at the camper. "Sir, it looks like there might be some room in there. Can we take turns riding in it?"

"Well, I figure it'd be tight in the truck and just left enough room for Curi in the camper. Let's say we make some more room in there and it should make the ride in the truck just a tad more comfortable."

Preech's eyes lit up, and he motioned me over so no one else could hear. "Go get Curi and take him for a walk behind the house. Say it's for a bathroom break."

"Okay. What's up?"

"Ohh, a good one just came to me. Make sure you take him quick, right before we load up."

"Roger that."

Preech walked over to Oliver. "Sir, do you mind if I grab some MRE's to take on the trip?"

"Hey, that's a heck of an idea. Go grab whatever you want."

Preech pointed to the back of the house, then tapped his watch before he scampered up the steps.

"I'll give Curi one more chance to go to the bathroom. Are we headin' out soon?"

Oliver looked at his watch. "In exactly thirteen minutes. Thanks for lookin' after him."

I walked Curi around back, and looked up to see Preech standing next to an open window. It was still dark, but I could make out an oval shape in his hand. He had a grin so big it sort of made him look like the Grinch. They had played a million pranks on each other, but I had only seen that look a few times before. Something told me he had come up with a doozy.

CHAPTER 12

"Whatcha got?" I whispered.

He tried to talk, but kept giggling and couldn't say anything.

I got close enough to see what was in his hands and almost died laughing. He was opening a can of Spam, one of Curi's most favorite things to eat. The only problem was it gave him paint-peeling, eye-watering, horrible gas. The last time he ate some, it was hours before we could get within ten feet of him. I was scared he was going to jump in the pond, let one loose, and pollute it forever.

Preech dumped the lumpy meat out of the can, and Curi chomped most of it before it hit the grass. Within ten seconds, there was nothing left. "Good dog," Preech whispered, then closed the window and locked it.

I walked him back to the camper and did my best not to laugh as he hopped in. The Oracle had emptied an area about the size of a shower stall. All of our stuff towered around the opening.

Rudy grabbed some of the MRE's Preech was carrying and jumped in with Curi.

Oliver looked at both of them and nodded his approval. "Well, we've got both tanks full of gas, and I want to chew up as much road as possible before we stop. You got everything you need in there?"

Rudy saluted. "Yes, sir."

Oliver closed the door, and checked to make sure it was secure. "Well, let's head out. Next stop, somewhere closer to the beach."

I hopped in the truck, and Preech took the seat by the door.

We were a few miles out of town, watching the sun paint yellow and purple streaks in the sky. Oliver sighed and reached for the box that held his eight-tracks. "Bein' on the open road sure is good for the soul. I wanted to surprise you boys with somethin', so take a look in here."

I opened the clasp and was very surprised by what was inside. "Man, this is cool. Where'd you get the Jimmy Buffett tape?"

"Record store. The most hippie thing I listened to before meeting you three was Lynyrd Skynyrd, but I can listen to that *He Went to Paris* song every day without gettin' tired of it."

Preech peered in the box. "Wow, and some KISS too. Thank you, sir."

"Well, that sounds like pots bangin' together to me, but y'all can plug it in if I'm not around. That's a little too hippie for me, but I figure you'll grow out of it someday. And speakin' of hippies, if y'all ever see one burnin' a flag, come and let me know where he is. Then just run along."

"Ten-four," I said.

Preech jabbed me in the ribs with his elbow. I looked at him and noticed he was trying hard to hold back a laugh. He nodded his head towards the side mirror, and I looked to see what he was talking about. Rudy's head was hanging out the camper window. His eyes were pinched shut, and his cheeks flapped like flags in the wind.

I tried not to laugh but couldn't help it. Once I got rolling, Preech couldn't hold back anymore and we both cracked up until tears ran down our faces.

Oliver smiled and looked at us. "What's so funny?

Preech cranked the truck window down. "It's that jokester Rudy. He's stickin' his head out the camper window, actin' the fool."

81

Oliver leaned over to get a look at the mirror. "Looks like he's tryin' to say something. Can you hear him?"

Preech poked his head out the window and cupped his hand to his ear. "What's that?" he yelled. "Ohh, okay, will do." He gave Rudy a thumbs up and closed the window.

"I couldn't hear him real good, but I think he said to thank you for the trip, and drive as far as we can to get there quicker."

"Well, sounds like a plan to me." Oliver said as he stepped on the gas.

We drove for hours, and every time Rudy's head poked out of the camper Preech and I died laughing.

Oliver took another look at the side mirror. "Maybe we should stop soon, he may be tryin' to tell us he needs to go to the bathroom or something."

Preech shook his head. "Maybe if we need gas or if you need somethin', sir. I think for a brainless wonder, Rudy is quite resourceful. I'm sure he has Coke bottles and stuff just in case."

"Good point. Plus we're makin' great time. It's the stops that kill ya."

After a while The Oracle yawned and stretched his arms. "Well, about time to refuel. It sure would be nice if y'all could drive a leg or two, but it won't be long before you can."

Preech raised his hand. "I'll give it a shot, sir."

"Don't let your folks know I told you this, but it doesn't take a license to drive a car, all it takes is a key. Maybe we'll start workin' on drivin' lessons when we get back."

Oliver saw a gas station and turned in. He whistled as we pulled up to the pumps. "Holy moley, they charge eighty-nine cents for a gallon of gas here. What the heck do they make it out of, bald eagle beaks?"

We laughed and hopped out as soon as he came to a stop. The door to the camper flew open, and Rudy slid out onto the concrete. He got on all fours and kissed the ground.

Preech and I walked to Rudy, and Oliver limped around the back of the camper. "You alright, son?"

"Ahh man, it was torture. I thought something had crawled in there and died until I figured out it was coming from Curi."

Oliver whistled, and Curi jumped out of the camper and ran to lick him. "Is he sick or something?"

"I wouldn't say he's sick, I just think he ain't right. Maybe it's the road trippin', 'cause he sure had some evil stuff eekin' out of him. I think my nose hairs are burnt."

Oliver rubbed Curi's head. "Did he sneak something to eat he shouldn't have?"

"No sir, I never got hungry enough to open any food. It was way too nasty in there."

"Well, he rides with me all over town and never has a problem."

"He got better about an hour ago. I think we're gonna have to unhitch the camper and burn it to the ground. There's no way we can get that smell out of everything. It reminded me of the day he ate some...hey, wait a minute."

Rudy's head whipped to Preech.

Preech had sucked both of his lips in to try to keep from laughing. He was biting down so hard it looked like he was wearing white lipstick.

"Well, punkenstein, do you have anything you need to say before I beat you into the ground?"

"Well, I umm, ha, ummm, hahahad thought it would be nice to feed Curi before we took off. I thought it was dog food, but, ummm, I might have grabbed the wrong thing, like Spam."

83

Oliver shook his head and laughed. "Well, at least now we know what it was. Let's open the windows on the camper to air it out the rest of the way, and stretch our legs some."

Rudy grabbed Preech's shirt collar. "I was going to take it easy on you this trip, weasel boy, but now it is on. Very on, so I wouldn't plan on sleeping, closing your eyes, or even blinking for the next few days."

Preech laughed and danced a jig. "Sorry man, I saw the shot and took it. You'd have done the same."

Rudy grinned and slowly nodded. "Dang skippy I would have."

I walked around the camper to see if Oliver needed any help. He was pumping gas and looking at the pile of stuff in the back of the truck. I looked as well, and it seemed like some things had blown out. We looked at each other, shrugged, and I walked into the gas station.

Preech and Rudy were staring at a big jar filled with pink liquid. Something familiar floated around inside it.

The attendant pointed to the jar. "How many pig's feet do y'all want?"

Rudy gagged, and Preech kept staring. "My buddy here is partial to pig snouts, or just live pigs, you got any of those?"

"Nope. But we got jerky and Cokes."

"That'll be great. Thank you, sir. Where exactly are we?"

"I noticed y'all had Texas plates and didn't pull up to the full service pumps. This here is Louisiana. And the name's Jeff."

Preech smiled and stuck out his hand. "Cool, Jeff. Good to meet ya. Do y'all got gators?"

"Yep. Everywhere. Do y'all got 'em?"

"Nope, not where we're from. But my other buddy there thought one had him the other day. It turned out to be fishing line with a catfish the size of a Buick on it. Has a gator ever got you?"

"Nah, but they've tried. If one comes after you, run in a zig-zag away from it. They ain't got kneecaps, so they can only run in a straight line. My cousin Lefty tried to run straight away from one once, but they are demon-quick. I can call him to come show you his stump if you want."

Preech's eyebrows shot up. "Umm, no, that's alright. We gotta get goin'. Good to know though, thanks."

We bought beef jerky and Cokes for us, and a new coffee cup for Oliver with an alligator and pelican on it.

Rudy was walking towards the camper, then took a hard left and headed for the truck. "I don't think I can ever even get in a camper again. That was nuts."

I smiled and patted him on the shoulder. "Hop up front with us, amigo. It'll be tight, but no problemo."

Curi was tied to the back bumper. He had crawled under the truck, pulling against his leash and barking his head off.

Preech leaned over to catch his attention. "Hey boy, what's up?" He stood and looked around. "Hey, do y'all see The Oracle?"

I took off to check out the camper, and Preech went to look inside the truck.

The sound of bottles crashing to the ground and Coke spraying everywhere made me jump. I turned to look at Rudy. He was staring open-mouthed at something next to the gas station, and pieces of everything he had been carrying glittered in the sunlight around him.

I followed his eyes, and when I saw what he was looking at, it felt like somebody had kneed me in the stomach. I didn't feel Oliver's mug slip out of my hand, but heard it bust into a million pieces on the concrete.

The Oracle was on the ground, motionless. There were two guys standing over him, and a huge knife was sticking straight up out of his leg.

CHAPTER 13

Rudy let out a scream like a banshee and took off towards The Oracle. His fists were white-knuckled in fury, and small rocks and dust sprayed up behind his sneakers. His legs churned so fast they were almost a blur.

I snapped out it and took off, with Preech right behind me. As we got closer, I could see the guys weren't much older than us. One of them was trying to talk to Oliver but had a weird look on his face, kind of like he was crying.

When Rudy got a few steps away, he launched into one of the guys and buried his shoulder into the punk's back. The vicious hit bent him like a rag doll and whipped him into his partner. Their heads hit so hard it sounded like coconuts banging together.

Rudy's momentum carried him over the guys, and after he hit the ground, he rolled once then hopped up with his fists in the air. He didn't need them, since both of the guys were knocked out cold.

I skidded to a stop and looked down at Oliver. "Are you okay, sir?"

"Well, I've been better, but I ain't hurt if that's what you're askin'. I was headin' to the outhouse, and these two bum-rushed me. Out of an old habit I did a blind leg sweep on 'em. I reckon I lost my balance and ended up on the ground."

Preech pointed to the knife that rose from Oliver's leg like a flagpole. "It looks like you lucked out with the leg they stabbed."

Oliver peered down at the knife. "You are correct, soldier. When I swept him, the knucklehead fell on his knife and it pegged my peg leg. Both of 'em freaked out when they saw what happened, and I think one of 'em was tryin' to apologize when Rudy knocked his block off."

Rudy stood over their bodies like they had stood over The Oracle. "So, do we beat 'em up?"

Oliver pushed himself to a sitting position. "Well, from the way that guy peed himself, I think it was their first and last heist. So I say we let them ride." He grunted as he pulled the knife from his leg. "We'll keep this to cut bait. It looks like a good kitchen knife, and I figure his momma will tan him good when she figures he took it."

We helped Oliver up and dusted him off. He looked at Rudy in awe. "Dang boy, you sure you don't wanna play linebacker instead of quarterback? That hit was one heck of a slobber-knocker."

Rudy shrugged. "Thank you, sir, but we'll see what the coach says. I just kinda flipped out when I saw those guys tryin' to hurt you. Nobody else will mess with you on our watch."

Oliver chuckled. "Well, good to hear. I told your folks it'd be me who'd keep an eye on y'all, but sometimes it's all hands on deck. Did ya pick up any snacks?"

Preech pointed his thumb towards the truck. "I bet the jerky made it, but I don't think the Cokes were all that lucky."

"Let's grab some more, then get on the road. We're burnin' too much daylight."

Preech and I walked next to The Oracle, and after a few steps I looked around until I found Rudy. He had stayed back and gave both of the guys a swift kick in the ribs before he jogged to catch up with us.

We entered the gas station and told Jeff what had happened. His eyes bugged out, and he ran outside.

He came back in shaking his head. "I saw them limpin' off, and it was exactly who I figured it'd be. Levi and Jimbo have been causin' trouble around here lately, but never anything like that."

Oliver flicked some dust off of his elbow. "Well, we gotta get the show back on the road, and I was thinkin' about letting the matter ride. You reckon I should call the authorities?"

Jeff smiled. "Well, you can kill two birds with one stone if you want. Levi's pop is the Chief of Police, and he would prob'ly want to hear about this. Jimbo moved to town not too long ago and don't look like he's a good guy to hang around with."

Oliver thought for a second, then pointed to the phone. "Do you mind ringin' the police department?"

Jeff picked up the handset and dialed a number from a list on the wall.

Oliver looked at us as he took the handset from Jeff. "It's like we talked about, boys. If you hang out with dogs, you get fleas."

Jeff waved his hand towards the snack aisle. "Hey boys, y'all feel free to get what got messed up out there. My treat."

We grabbed more Cokes and another mug for Oliver.

When we got back to the register, Oliver winked at us as he talked. "Yes, that's what happened, and I'll come down there this instant and put my hand on a stack of Bibles if need be."

I heard a voice on the other end of the line but couldn't make out what he was saying.

Oliver cleared his throat to answer. "Retired Army, sir. On our way from Texas to Florida with a fine crew of youngsters to do some divin' and fishin'."

The voice on the phone sounded louder, but I still couldn't hear what he was saying.

After a few minutes Oliver smiled and answered. "Yes, I knew him well. An excellent man to serve under. Well, we better be scootin'. I'll leave Jeff here my number back home, and look me up if you're ever down my way."

He hung up the phone. "Well, that's two boys who are gonna get hammered so hard they ain't gonna be able to sit for a week. Let's get movin'."

We ran back to the truck, and Rudy was the first one in the cab. I jumped in after him, making sure to sit between him and Preech. If they sat next to each other, it would be like putting a lit match next to a box of dynamite.

As we rolled out of the parking lot, Oliver pointed to the glove box. "Would one of you mind grabbin' the map?"

Preech reached in and pulled out the wadded mess. We had tried to refold it at Oliver's house, but the best we got looked like a crumpled soccer ball.

"I know that stop hung some time on us, but how are we lookin?"

Preech traced his finger over the map. "Well, if we're in Louisiana, it looks like we gotta get through Mississippi and Alabama. Then we drive into Florida a while, take a right, then a left, then a right and we're there."

He looked up and grinned at Oliver. "Accordin' to the map, we only got about eight inches to go."

Oliver laughed. "Well, I like the sound of that. I figure we're close to halfway, so we should get there sometime tonight or early mornin' tomorrow. If the weather cooperates, y'all should be divin' on the wreck sometime tomorrow afternoon."

"Woo-hoo," we said as we high fived each other.

Preech pointed at the telephone poles, which stood like sentries along the highway. "Wouldn't it be cool if we could have telephones in our cars? Then people could call you if they needed something at the store. You'd just stop on the way instead of getting all the way home then havin' to turn around to go back."

"I know you're a fart smeller, I mean smart feller, and all Preech, but that has to be one of the dumbest things I've ever heard you say," Rudy replied.

"Do you know how long the cord would have to be to plug in the wall and stretch all the way from home to where somebody works? Would you have to wind it up every night? And what if some other truck snags the cord on the bumper and it rips your arm off while you're talking on it?"

"No, more like a walkie talkie," explained Preech. "Like using air waves or gamma rays or whatever they use."

"Oh, that would be just beautiful," said Rudy. "Since there is only like a twenty-foot range, someone would have to be parked in the garage when you call to tell him to go back to the store. Just brilliant, Preech, brilliant."

"Stranger things have happened, boys. Some fella could make a bucket of money if he figured something like that out. It never hurts to think about things," said Oliver.

We flew past a hitchhiker. He was sitting on the side of the road, sunburned to a dark red glow.

"Do y'all know what Ted does to hitchhikers?"

I bit my lip as I waited for the reply.

"He stops, all nice like, and says, 'Hey buddy, you tired of walkin'?' When they say yes, he laughs and tells them to run. Then he peels out and sprays gravel on 'em."

Preech let a breath out, making his lips loose so it sounded like a motorboat. "Man, I know respectin' parents is one of the Ten Commandments and all, but that's hard to do with that guy."

"Yeah," Rudy said. "I wished I lived in Washington, D.C., 'cause my mom says instead of the Ten Commandments, all they got there is the three suggestions."

Oliver's laughter boomed around the truck. "Well son, she might be right about that, but I am concerned Ted is crossin' some lines. Would you like me to ask my police friends to talk to him? Or I'd be more than happy to pay him a visit."

"Thanks, but Mom says she's gonna try to get a doctor to fix him up, if he'll go talk to one. I don't like y'all havin' to deal with my garbage, and I can't do anything anyway. I appreciate it though."

"Well, if you say you cain't do somethin', it's pretty near a fact you ain't gonna do it. Don't sell yourself short, because I think there's an answer for everything no matter how hard it seems."

I could tell Rudy was uncomfortable by the way he squirmed in his seat. "Yessir, I think I know what you're sayin', but it seems like something y'all don't gotta mess with."

Oliver pointed his finger in the air. "But that's what buddies are for. Friends come in and out of your life like flies at a picnic, and may even come bail you outta jail. But a buddy will be sittin' next to you in the cell sayin', 'Dang, that was fun.'"

We nodded our agreement.

"Just keep me posted on what I can do to help."

"Yessir, will do."

"By the way, how'd the three of y'all meet?"

Preech smiled and pointed his thumb at Rudy. "By saving this brainiac from getting pummeled into a speck of dust on his first day of third grade."

"How's that?"

"Well, he shows up with a Pittsburgh Steelers tee shirt. Everyone at our school is either a Dallas Cowboys or Houston Oilers fan. That's it. Period."

"Yep, he was surrounded and about to get hammered. Then Preech invented a game called Trip the Weasel to get everyone doin' somethin' else, and I snuck Rudy into school to get a new shirt."

Preech rubbed his chin. "I think about that sometimes, and wonder what a beautiful place the world would be if I was out of school with the flu or bubonic plague that day."

Oliver chuckled. "Boy, you two would have a lot more time on your hands if that were the case."

"You bet I would...no tellin' what I'd have invented by now if my number one daily task wasn't payin' back el bone head. Which reminds me Oliver, do you mind holdin' my hose while I'm divin'? I don't want that gorilla within ten miles of it."

Rudy grinned and made cricket noises with his tongue.

"I think I can handle that, Trooper. Hey Rudy, how'd y'all get to Texas anyway?"

"Well, I grew up in Pennsylvania, and one day my real dad got accidentally stomped to death by a bunch of runaway Amish horses."

The truck got so quiet it hurt my ears. I knew something happened to his dad, but we'd never talked about it.

"The Amish folks kept bringin' food and furniture they made to say sorry, but it started to drive my mom crazy. So one day she covered her eyes and poked a map on a wall. She hit Texas, so we sold everything that didn't fit in the car and took off."

We drove in silence until I saw two 5,000 gallon tanks in the corner of a pasture. "Look at that. Someone painted "GAS ONLY" on that one and "WATER ONLY" on the other one. You reckon somebody got mixed up before?"

Oliver grinned. "Yep, looks like it. You're in a world of hurt if you put water in your tractor gas tank, or use gas to water your crops. And the way they spray painted five lines under each word looks like they were pretty angry."

He picked up his new coffee cup and admired it. "Rudy, do you mind grabbin' some of that newspaper on the dash and wrappin' this up. Then put it under the seat for safe keepin'."

"Will do."

Rudy carefully wrapped the cup and slid it under the seat. He pulled his hand out, and one of his fingers was covered with fluffy white goo.

"Oops, sorry Oliver. Did I poke your fire extinguisher or somethin'?"

"Nope, unless fire extinguisher innards taste like coconut cream pie. Give it a whirl."

Rudy licked his finger. "Dang, if fire extinguisher stuff tastes this good, I'm gonna suck every one of 'em dry when we get back to school."

Oliver laughed. "Well, I wouldn't advise that. A couple of my lady friends gave me pies for the trip. I was gonna surprise y'all on the beach with 'em."

I thought about the nice ladies, but shuddered when I remembered of Miss Fenton. "They sure are high on you Oliver, like they all want to marry you or somethin'. What's your secret?"

Oliver took his hands off the steering wheel for a second and held them up like he was surrendering. "I've figured out a lot of stuff, but I'm as sharp as a marble when it comes to the prettier species. I think if you respect 'em and treat 'em right, you'll do okay."

Preech's eyes got big and he started to talk with his hands. "My cousin said he saw a pretty girl at the mall and walked up to her and asked her what her sign was. And she just looked at him, said 'Closed', then walked away."

"Ouch." Oliver said. "You know boys, I read something once that said a man's body is like a tool, but every lady's body is a work of art. Just some of them are on bigger pieces of canvas than others. Think about that and you'll do the right thing."

I looked at The Oracle. "Do you reckon you'll ever get married?"

He thumped his fingers on the steering wheel and took so long to answer I didn't think he'd heard me. "Well, it did happen once, but it's a very, very long story. Maybe someday I'll fill y'all in." Oliver sighed and turned up the radio as Johnny Cash's song *Sunday Morning Coming Down* drifted out of it.

Little did we know the answer to that story would change everything we knew about our world.

CHAPTER 14

We got to the beach just as the sun was coming up. The sand was as white as sugar and the water was a clear, clean green.

Preech laughed and pointed at Rudy. "Hey, that water's the same color as your face when you chewed some of Oliver's Levi Garrett."

"Zip it, shrimp boy. I think a knuckle sandwich will keep your yap from flappin'."

"Well Troopers, my buddy Sam said to get our camp set up and meet him a little after noon. What say y'all get the tent set up, and I'll take Curi for a walk before unhookin' the trailer and helpin' y'all unpack."

We grabbed the tent, and since we'd put it up once at Oliver's, it only took a few minutes to get it ready to go.

Rudy looked at the pile in the back of the truck. "Well fellas, what say we start pulling stuff out, but leave in our divin' and fishin' things."

We nodded and unpacked most of the truck. There were so many things it looked like we planned to stay for a month.

Oliver came back, and Curi gave each of us a big slobbery lick. "Well boys, I'm tuckered out from the drive. If you help me unhook the trailer, I think I'm gonna take a bit of a siesta before we meet up with Sam."

"Yessir, what would you like us to do during the siesta?"

"Looks like y'all are doing a good job getting everything set up, so once that's done, run around and have fun. Just stay close and make sure you wake me up around noon."

Preech dropped the shovel in his hand to set the alarm on his watch. "Will do."

Oliver bent over and whispered, "And try to keep those two from killin' each other...I kinda promised their folks I'd get 'em back in one piece."

"Ten-four," I whispered back.

We organized the campsite, dug a fire pit, and went over our diving plan.

Preech was checking his list. "We got leather gloves for dive gloves?"

"Check," I said as I held up two pairs.

"Empty sacks to put stuff in?"

"Check."

"Empty sacks for sand bags?"

"Check."

I glanced over at Rudy and watched a grin slide across his face as he eyed the sacks. Preech went over the rest of the list and I smiled too, and tried to guess what Rudy was up to.

Oliver came out of the camper just as Preech's alarm went off, and we almost didn't recognize him. He had on a bright Hawaiian shirt, pants, and a big straw hat.

Preech whistled. "Look out ladies. The man, the myth, the legend—Oliver—has arrived."

Oliver smiled and bowed. "Well divers, are y'all ready to get wet?"

"Let's roll!" yelled Preech.

We helped Oliver with the directions his friend had given him and wound up at a marina. There were more boats than I even knew existed—great big white ones longer than a bus and sailboats every color of the rainbow.

Oliver saw Sam, and they hugged and slapped each other on the back.

Sam's hair was as white as George Washington's, and he had a big smile like Oliver. "So this is your posse? Looks like a great crew."

We greeted Sam and shook his hand like The Oracle had taught us.

"Well, look at that. Youngsters with manners and respect. It's sad how hard that is to find these days."

Oliver beamed. "These are the best kids—I mean young men—in the county. I guarantee you they'll say or do somethin' today you'll never forget."

"Well, I'm lookin' forward to it. Y'all ready to push off?"

Preech saluted Sam. "Aye, aye, Captain. That sure is a nice boat. How long is it?"

"I secured us an eighteen-footer, and it's got plenty of zip to get us there." He winked at Oliver. "And plenty of storage space for the pirate treasure y'all find."

We loaded our stuff into the boat Sam had tied to a dock, then climbed aboard as Sam cranked the engine then eased us through the marina. Once we got clear of the buoys, Sam punched it and we flew across the water. There were hardly any waves, and the bluish-green water stretched on forever. I wondered how many millions of fish were all around us, just waiting to get caught.

After about twenty minutes, Sam eased up the throttle and came to a stop. He tapped some gauges, scratched his head, then cruised another few minutes before he cut off the engines.

"Well, there she is boys. Get after it."

I looked into the shimmering water and could see dark shapes scattered across the ocean floor. Some of the pieces of the ship looked as big as cars, and others were the size of treasure chests.

Since there were only two sets of diving equipment, we played rock-paper-scissors to see who went down first. Preech and I won, and I could barely contain my excitement as I got into the water.

I put the mask on, and Rudy rolled out enough slack in the garden hose to get me to the ocean floor. He smiled as he handed me the sack we'd half-filled with sand, and I gave him a thumbs up before I grabbed it and let it take me into the deep.

It took me to the bottom pretty fast, but I landed on my feet and thought to not put as much sand in the next time. I looked around, feeling like I'd just landed on another planet. Hundreds of small fish were darting around me and the pieces of the ship. I never knew so many different kinds and colors of fish existed—they were almost too pretty to use for bait.

The wreckage looked like a treeless cemetery where someone had kicked over all of the tombstones. The sand that covered everything was like a weird dust and reminded me of nuclear fallout in the films they showed us at school.

I saw something round and white in the sand, and was sure it was the back of a pirate's skull. Just as I bent over to pick it up, something whizzed down beside me. It was Preech, and his crash caused a huge sandy upside-down mushroom cloud.

Once the sand settled, I couldn't hold back a laugh that exploded into a million bubbles. Preech was holding his sack, which had fallen sideways and spilled sand everywhere. Obviously Rudy had packed Preech's sack extra full. I remembered Rudy's smile when we checked the sacks off the list and grinned as I sucked another breath down the hose.

Preech adjusted his mask, dumped out the extra sand, and stood as he shook his fist back towards the boat. He screamed something into the hose, and I couldn't understand him but was sure he'd never say it in church. Rudy looked down at us, and through the shimmer I could see him smile and do a little wave with his fingers.

I bent to pick up the skull, hoping it was still connected to the pirate skeleton with diamond rings attached to every skeleton finger. It came out easily, mostly because it wasn't attached to anything, and because it wasn't even a skull. It turned out to be one of the coolest seashells I'd ever seen, so I stuck it in an empty sack tied to a belt loop on my cutoff jean shorts.

It was like I had gone deaf but could hear things better than I ever could. My ears felt like they could feel things instead of hear them, and each bubble I breathed out carried a different tune with it.

Preech was a few steps ahead of me. He dug through the sand and put stuff in the sack he had tied to his shorts.

I bent over and sifted through the sand as well, and knew I'd see bright gold coins any second. I found some chunks of metal, and I slipped them into my bag, totally sure they were gold or silver that had rusted over and would be worth millions.

Preech screamed again, and I figured Rudy had slipped a sand crab or something into his hose. When I looked at Preech, his eyes were as big as tennis balls. I glanced up, and terror clawed into my chest when I realized I was staring at the belly of a shark as long as our boat.

CHAPTER 15

Preech nudged up against me and grabbed my arm so hard his fingernails dug into my skin. I thought of letting go of the sand bag but was scared I'd float up like a big piece of fish food for the shark to chomp.

Preech was trying to yell something to me, but all I could hear was my heart boom like it was about to crack through my ribs. It sounded like somebody hitting a huge drum, using human leg bones as drumsticks.

We watched the shark swim away, and I prayed it would keep going. All hope disappeared when the beast whipped around, coming back towards the boat. Its massive head moved back and forth, like it smelled something for lunch and hadn't found it yet.

Preech and I backed up against part of the wreckage about the size of a coffin. I hugged Preech and pulled him down to a crouch, and thought that if we made ourselves as small as possible the creature wouldn't see us. We pushed back against the spiky wood and did our best to hide behind the sand bags.

He passed over us again and was so big his body blotted out the sun as he floated by. I could see the guys in the boat yelling and smacking the water with an oar. I guessed they were trying to scare him off.

My head started to swirl like I was going to pass out, then I realized I had stopped breathing. I slowly let my breath out, but I was scared the bubbles would catch the shark's attention.

I tried to look away but couldn't take my eyes off of him. The awesomeness of the creature made me follow its every flinch. He cruised through the water like a torpedo made out of muscles.

As the shark passed the boat, Preech pointed to the sack in his hand. I figured he wanted to let go and make a break for it, but I shook my head 'no' since I knew we couldn't out-swim the ocean's perfect predator.

The shark turned again, this time swimming a little deeper, about halfway between us and the boat. I was terrified it was going to get tangled in our hoses and drag us around like big slabs of bait, but it somehow slithered through them.

He swam further away than before, and I was about to give Preech a sign to drop his bag so we could try to make it to the boat. Just as I raised my finger, the shark took a quick turn and zoomed directly at us.

His death black eyes stared right into mine. He opened and closed his jaws, like he was checking to make sure they worked.

I shoved my hand into every hole in the chunk of boat we were backed up against, praying I'd find something to use as a weapon.

Something clamped onto me, and pain shot from my fingers all the way up my arm. I figured it was a big ugly eel, trying to chew my fingers off while the shark feasted on the rest of me. I yanked my hand out, surprised to see a blue crab the size of a lobster attached to it. If I didn't have the work gloves on, it felt like the crab would have pinched my fingers clean off.

The shark was so close I could count every jagged tooth in his mouth when I pushed the crab toward his massive gray snout.

The surge of water the shark created was so strong it shoved me against the wreckage, where barnacles and shards of wood bit into my back. The diving mask flew off my face, and I was blinded by an underwater storm of sand and water the shark had kicked up. In a split second, the crab, my glove, and the beast had disappeared into the murky blue.

The salt water scorched my eyes, but I could make out a blurry Preech next to me. He was wiggling like a giant worm, trying to burrow into his sand bag. I grabbed him by the back of the shirt with one hand, and used the other to find his hand and peel his fingers off of the bag. The other guys must have seen what was going on, because the second I found one of the hoses, we flew off the ocean floor towards the boat.

Within seconds, Preech and I were laid out on the deck, coughing up seawater and trying to rub the sting out of our eyes. Sam, Rudy, and Oliver stood over us, breathing as hard as we were from pulling us back into the boat.

Sam broke the silence. "Dang Oliver, you were right. I ain't never gonna forget today."

Rudy pointed to my bleeding fingers. "You all right Kev man? Did he get you?"

I bolted upright and looked at my fingers, then counted them over and over to make sure they were all there. "It was crazy. This big crab tried to pinch my fingers off, then the shark ate it and my glove and took off."

Sam dug a first aid kit out of a locker and handed it to me. I found a piece of gauze, cut it into strips, and wrapped my fingers like I'd seen Gramps wrap his when he had hooked himself.

Oliver sighed. "Boy, was I worried about you two. We did all we could to chase it away, but it just kept comin' back."

Sam patted Rudy on the back. "This is one heck of an amigo y'all got here. It took all I had to keep him from jumpin' on that critter to rescue you two."

"Well, I was gonna get down there and throw Kevin back in the boat, then stick some tuna fish down Preech's britches and hop back in the boat myself."

Preech's mouth made a weak grin. "Not if that poor critter caught a whiff of you. It would have eaten himself from the tail up to get away from such nastiness."

We sat in silence, looking out over smooth rolling waves. It had all happened so fast—I felt like it was some kind of weird dream.

"Well Troopers, are y'all ready to head back in? Curi's got plenty of food and water but is prob'ly going nuts being tied to the trailer. And I bet we can get some bay fishin' in...if y'all feel up to it."

I gave him the best smile I could. "Yessir, that would be great."

Sam cranked the engine and we roared towards the marina. The hot air felt excellent against my skin, but I shivered most of the way back.

"That is the biggest tiger shark I've ever seen around here. They say the sharks own the water, we just rent it now and then," hollered Sam over the whine of the engine.

Oliver patted me on the back. "Boy, I'm glad that ended like it did. It must have been terrifyin' down there."

I yelled so he could hear me over the wind and boat noise. "It was the weirdest thing ever, totally scary but very cool at the same time...like Miss Fenton's head on Marilyn Monroe's body."

Oliver started laughing so hard he almost rolled out of the boat.

We got back to the marina, said our goodbyes to Sam, and drove to the campsite. Curi was covered in sand and did his best to rub it off on us as he jumped and welcomed everyone back.

"Hey, I forgot to ask, did you boys get any treasure down there?"

Preech snapped his fingers. "Nope, but there was some pretty cool stuff." He grabbed his sack and emptied it in the back of the truck.

"Here's some pieces of wood, metal chunks, and these cool rocks." Preech counted the handful of golf ball-sized rocks in his hand. "Looky there, one for each of us. I say we call 'em lucky rocks, because I feel luckier today than I ever have." He tossed one to each of us.

I caught mine and scratched at the tar coating on the jagged black stone then stuck it in my pocket. "When you think about it, being lucky rocks, too. It doesn't rock as hard as KISS, but nothing rocks as hard as KISS."

Everyone except Oliver nodded in approval.

I pulled the shell out of my bag and buried all but the top of it in the sand. "That's what this looked like when I found it. I hoped it was a skull, but no dice. I got some metal stuff too, maybe it's gold that rusted over."

I held up a chunk of the metal, and as I squeezed it, the glob turned into rusty dust in my hand. I brushed my fingers off on my shorts and noticed some pencil eraser-sized drops of blood had seeped through the bandage on my fingers. I got my bag out of the tent, tore off a strip of clean T-shirt, and re-wrapped my wounds.

I made sure no one was looking, then looked up at the cloudless sky and whispered, "Thanks for everything you taught me, and thanks for helpin' with that shark, too."

I walked back to the truck where Rudy was unloading a crab trap Sam had loaned us. It was square and about as big as a school desk, made of rubber-coated chicken wire.

Oliver pointed to a latch on the top. "That's where the bait goes. Let's go catch some fish, then put the innards in there."

Preech scratched his head. "How does this thing work?"

"The crabs go through the holes in the sides, and once they swim in, they cain't swim back out. We'll leave the trap in one spot, then go deeper in the bay to fish for a while. When we come back, we might have a mess of crabs to eat with the fish we catch."

Preech pointed to a package covered in white butcher paper. "While y'all were loadin' up, Sam gave me that. He said it'd be great bait for the trap."

Oliver opened the package and smiled. "Well, well, ain't he a champ? This here is chicken necks and beef tongues, some of the best bait you can use because it holds together so good under water."

Preech looked around. "Sam said to chop it up some to fit in the trap. Where's the bait knife we got in Louisiana?"

Oliver pointed at Rudy. "Your compadre there stabbed the shark with it."

I smiled and looked at Rudy. "What a stallion! Did you stick it in him?"

"Naw. I tried, but that sharkskin is tough. I waited for him to come close to the boat and stuck it as hard as I could. It sounded like a baseball hittin' a catcher's mitt, but he didn't even flinch. The knife slipped out of my grip and I lost it in the water."

Preech raised his hand. "I vote you swim out there and get it, along with the sacks of sand Kev and I left behind. Chop chop, bait boy, time's a wastin'."

Oliver opened his tackle box and pulled out a filet knife in a leather sheath. "I think we'll manage, fellas. You can use this knife, Preech. Why don't you two get the rods rigged up, and I'll get the other stuff ready."

I opened my tackle box, and the sight of all the cool saltwater tackle sent a tingle down my back. "Are we gonna fish the bottom, or should we use poppin' corks?"

Oliver rubbed the grey and black stubble on his chin. "How 'bout half of us fish top and the other two fish the bottom. That a way we can all switch when we see what they're hittin'."

"Ten-four. Can you coach me on the cast net? That's the coolest thing ever."

"You betcha. They say if you give a man a fish, he eats for a day. You teach a man to fish, and he gets a dang good excuse to drink beer all day long."

CHAPTER 16

We laughed and rigged the poles, then stacked everything in the back of the truck. Curi jumped up on the tailgate and wagged his tail. He nodded like he approved of our pack job and looked happy he wasn't going to get left behind.

Oliver drove down the sandy paths through the salt grass and stopped where the path ended. The dark green water went on forever and looked like humongous snakes that wound around the emerald green grass islands.

Oliver baited the crab trap and pointed to a spot in the water. "That should be a great place fellas. Just take this piece of plastic pipe and hammer it in, then tie the trap to it."

We were about to step in when Preech stopped in his tracks. "So, we're gonna walk in there with this thing drippin' with bait blood?"

Oliver looked at us, then out at the water. "Well fellas, I understand if it's too soon since the shark episode, but sometimes you gotta get back on a horse that bucked ya. The good news is it's only a couple of feet deep in most places, so there's no way a monster shark can be here without seein' him comin'."

Preech gulped and stepped forward, and we stepped in behind him.

Once we set the crab trap, we headed back towards Oliver. He had pulled everything out of the back of the truck and got the cast net ready to do its thing. His first throw sailed into a perfect circle and dove into the water next to a clump of salt grass. He pulled it in and dumped out shrimp, small blue crabs, and some other kind of silver fish onto the sand.

"All of that's good bait boys. Get it in the bait buckets. The long silver fish are mullet, and the ones that look like perch are called piggy perch. Redfish love 'em."

Preech picked up a shrimp, and Rudy howled and laughed when it flipped its head and impaled Preech's thumb with the long pointed horn on its head.

"Boys, everything out here has teeth, claws, or fins. Watch out where you touch 'em."

Preech shook his finger until the shrimp plopped into the bucket. "Oliver, do they got stingrays here like at the coast in Texas?"

"You betcha. Which reminds me that y'all need to shuffle when you walk in the water. They'll get out of your way if you kick 'em, but if you step right on top of 'em they're liable to nail you with their tail."

Rudy scratched his head. "So they whip you with the tail, like a lion tamer?"

"No, their tails got a barb on it. Goes in smooth, but flares out like a little Christmas tree. I've seen it make a three hundred pound Marine cry, so shuffle, shuffle, shuffle Troopers."

We stared wide-eyed at each other, then out over the peaceful green bay. I wondered how come the water wasn't boiling with so many angry critters living in it.

We set up Oliver's fishing platform, and he clapped and smiled as we handed him the small ice chest to set under his seat. It was full of Schlitz, his favorite beer.

He pushed off into the water a few feet, then turned around and held his push pole like a sword. He touched each of our shoulders like they did knights in the movies. "I anoint you Preech, knight of invention. You are Rudy, knight of the valiant fight, and Kevin, knight of peace."

We bowed and watched him cruise into the water. He stopped and pointed to something. "See those ripples, boys? Redfish. A whole mess of 'em. Throw your bait a few feet in front of 'em, then hold on."

I zinged my popping cork with a shrimp on the hook as far as I could, and it landed in front of the surging water. It bobbed around for a few seconds, then disappeared. I remembered what The Oracle said about waiting for a count of three to set the hook, since all of the ocean fish had extra-bony mouths so you had to wait for them take the bait real good before setting the hook.

The fish yanked so hard my pole almost flew out of my hand. I was glad I had held on, since there was no way I'd dive in after it with so many vicious fish and crabs everywhere. The power of the monster reminded me of the giant catfish, but it pulled ten times faster.

Rudy yelled. "I got one!"

"Me too," smiled Preech.

We landed our first redfish together. They were long and sleek, like someone had taken a bass, stretched it out three feet, then took the lips and puckered them like a perch. The golden and red scales blinded me in the sunlight, and each fish had a black spot on its tail.

Oliver poled his way back to us. "Nice reds, boys. They'll eat great. Put them on my stringer if you want. Just make sure to tie it back with a slip knot. If a shark or salt water gator grabs the fish, I can release it and let 'em take the fish. It's better to give 'em a meal than become one."

Rudy looked at Oliver. "You mean there's gators in the bay too?"

"Oh heck yeah. If one grabs the stringer, that sucker can pull you to Cuba if you don't have a way to undo the stringer—" Oliver stopped talking when he noticed Preech staring at him, his eyelid gearing up for full-twitch mode.

"Umm, what I meant to say was it's smart to have a quick release on the fish just in case. This is pretty skinny water, and I doubt there's any monster gators like the big ones out in the open ocean."

Rudy jabbed Preech in the calf with the tip of his pole, and Preech exploded out of the water. Rudy laughed until he couldn't breathe.

Curi was tied to the truck about a hundred yards away, and I could hear him bark as he cheered us on.

I pulled up the long piece of rope tied to Oliver's raft and poked the metal piece on the tip through a lip on the fish. Then I put them back in the water and re-tied the stringer into a slip knot Oliver could reach if he had to.

I grabbed my pole, baited my hook with a shrimp again, and threw it out as far as I could. The bobber floated around a while, then slowly started going against the current.

"Hey Kevin, that may be a flounder pullin' on your line. They tend to chew on the bait before they suck it in, so wait a bit then pull with all you got."

I waited for a count of five, then yanked back on my rod. The fish pulled hard as well but nothing like the redfish. When I brought it in, I grabbed my line and eased the fish out of the water.

I held it up and looked at The Oracle. "This thing is as flat as a pancake. Did a boat run over it or somethin'?"

Oliver laughed. "Nope. That's how flounders look. They are some of the best eatin' fish in the ocean. Make sure you get him on the stringer and try to get another one.

We fished for hours, and each of us caught redfish, flounder, and speckled trout.

"Well Troopers, it's gettin' close to dark, and I reckon we should leave some fish for the next guy. Let's run the crab trap and head back to the campsite."

We shuffled back to the trap and lifted it out of the water.

Oliver eased his platform next to us. "Hot dog, we hit the mother lode. Must be twenty of 'em in there."

I stared at the pile of sapphire-colored crabs as they snapped their claws at each other and the sides of the trap. I wondered if the crab that saved me from the shark was related to one of the crabs in the trap.

We dragged it through the water and back to the truck. Preech constantly looked around, for shark fins and gator backs I guessed.

Oliver helped us repack everything in the back of the truck. "Alright fellas, go ahead and clean the fish here and we can bait the trap with fish innards for the night. We may have a hundred in there by mornin'."

Preech saluted him. "Aye, aye, sir. You reckon we should tie Rudy the squidhead to the trap as well, to protect it from poachers and stuff tonight?"

"Well, let's get the fish cleaned and figure that out later. While you're at it, check the stomachs of the fish to see what they've been eatin' so we know what bait to use next time."

Like Oliver had taught us, we cut the meat fillets out of each fish, put them in plastic bags, then set them in the ice chest.

We got back to the campsite and turned on the lanterns.

"You got a good fire pit dug there boys. What you wanna do now is get some straight driftwood, a little bigger than a pool stick if you can find it. Take flashlights, and be extra careful."

We walked into the inky blackness into the sand dunes. Our flashlight beams were like light sabers that sliced through the night.

111

Preech pointed his flashlight to the sky and put his fingers over the top of it. It was like an X-ray, his bones a dark shadow and the pink blood cruised around them. "Man, it's a good thing that shark didn't get your hand, Kev man. You would have saved all kinds of money only havin' to buy one glove at a time, but that woulda been a bummer."

We found what we thought would work and dragged it back to the campsite. Oliver had a fire roaring from some firewood he'd brought from the farm. "Good job, Troopers. Now take some balin' wire and tie the wood pieces into big X's. Then hammer 'em in on both sides of the fire and put that metal bar across so we can hang our cookin' pot on it.

We drove the driftwood pieces into the sand with the back of the hatchet and secured them with the wire. We connected the metal rod across the fire, and Oliver hung a pot on it. He cooked the fish in beer, butter, lemon juice, salt, and pepper.

"Now, I've got the pot of water boilin' on the camp stove. The crabs are in that big bucket with an aerator on it...you gotta keep 'em alive 'till you boil them."

Preech scratched his chin. "Boy, that sounds like a heck of a way to go."

"Yep, I reckon it is. Do y'all know how to keep a crab in a bucket?"

Rudy grinned. "You put a pair of Preech's underwear next to it? That poor critter would rather sit there and starve to death than have to touch those."

Oliver chuckled. "Naw, you put more in. One crab might scuttle right out, but if there's more than one crab they'll reach up and pull the one tryin' to get out back in. It's kinda like people. Some'll lift you up, some'll pull you down...somethin' to think about when you figure out who's a friend and who ain't."

We used a long pair of tongs to grab the crabs and dropped them in the frothy boiling water.

"Okay boys, let them cook about ten minutes, then we'll turn the gas off and let 'em finish out."

Preech punched the alarm on his watch. "I'm on it, sir."

We took the pot with the fish off the fire, and as it cooled, we pulled the crabs out of the boiling water. I was amazed that they had changed from dark blue to a deep cherry red.

"Time to chow, boys. Just wrap the fish in a tortilla, and crack the crabs open with a hammer on the tailgate to get the meat out of them."

We ate until I couldn't take another bite, then Oliver got a pie from the truck and cut it into four pieces and put one on each of our plates. He ate his off of the tin foil pie plate.

"Thanks to dear, sweet Phyllis. She's won the county fair with this coconut cream pie recipe four years in a row."

I somehow got every bite of pie down, and we all collapsed into lawn chairs and stared at the fire. Our shadows danced behind us like ghostly black belly dancers.

"What's the number one thing you need to survive if you get stranded in the wild, boys?"

A piece of wood popped in the fire, like it was trying to answer Oliver's question.

"Food?" asked Rudy.

"Nope, but that one's up there," Oliver answered.

"Water?" I guessed.

"Nope, but that's closer." Oliver said.

Preech grinned. "Is it beer?"

Oliver laughed. "Nope, but I like the way you think, soldier. Actually, it's attitude. First you get the right attitude in your head you're gonna make it, then the quicker you'll be able to find shelter, water, food, and a way out. All of which gets you back to the beer."

The wind stopped blowing, and the buzz of mosquitoes filled the air.

Oliver winked at Rudy. "Did you bring any of that mosquito stuff you were talking about, Private Rudy?"

Rudy perked up and smiled. He cut his eyes at Preech, who was staring at a mosquito on his arm. Preech smashed it then studied the blood spot on his hand.

"Yessir, I did. I'll go get it."

Rudy had told me and Oliver about a prank he had planned on Preech and to make sure we would only use the stuff with the green lid. I remembered him saying, "Green is go, red is no."

Rudy carried two large jars of clear liquid towards the campfire and passed one over Preech's shoulder. Preech took the lid off and sniffed it. "So, do you just dip some on your shirt and rub it on?"

Rudy shook his head. "Nope, it takes a bunch to work. Pour some in your hand and lay it on thick, like this." He opened the jar with the green lid, poured it into his palm like a bowl, and spread it on his arms and legs.

Preech shrugged and did the same.

Nothing happened for a few seconds, then I could almost feel the wind from the wings of millions of kamikaze bloodsuckers. It was like they came from all over the county to get a piece of Preech.

CHAPTER 17

With every blink, more and more mosquitoes blanketed Preech and covered him so completely it looked like he was wearing a black diver's suit. "Holy cow, they're tryin' to carry me off...like the monkeys in the *Wizard of Oz!*"

I looked at Oliver, and his mouth hung open as he stared at Preech.

Rudy laughed and pointed his thumb towards the surf. "Hey bearded lady, you might wanna go wash 'em off."

Preech bolted for the water, and Oliver looked at Rudy, his eyebrows arched in amazement. "What the heck is in that?"

Rudy shrugged. "I dunno. Ted is always tryin' to make moonshine or somethin' in the garage, and when I was gettin' my campin' stuff I saw one of the jars was open and had about a million dead mosquitoes in it."

"Well young man, you may want to figure out exactly what he put in there. The army would love to hear about such a thing to use as a weapon. Nothing can break the enemy down faster than usin' nature against 'em."

Rudy's smile drooped into a frown. "Well, we ain't exactly talkin' right now."

Guilt ripped through me. I'd got to look for treasure, catch huge fish, and mess around on the beach and hadn't even thought about helping Rudy. I swore to myself I'd figure out something before we got back home.

Rudy's smile came back when he pointed a flashlight into the rolling waves, which caught Preech in mid-dunk as he splashed and slapped himself to get out of his insect overcoat.

"The stuff we put on us is repellent I got at the store. Do you reckon it'll keep 'em off mosquito boy when he gets back?"

Oliver chuckled. "He may have to gargle it or somethin', but the other stuff should wear off sometime."

Rudy carefully put the red lid back on the jar of stuff Preech had used, and wrapped it with foil. "I'm gonna set this under the backseat of the truck and make sure the windows are closed extra tight."

Preech came back from the water, trying to dig the last of the critters from his nose and ears. "What the heck happened? They're not even messin' with y'all. Did I not use enough Magic Juice?"

Rudy handed him the jar with the green lid. "No you didn't, knucklehead. You gotta lay this on extra, extra thick."

Preech warily opened the jar and sniffed the liquid. I dipped my finger in and rubbed it off on my arm and smiled. Preech nodded and poured some of it in both hands, then coated himself with it. Rudy snuck up behind him and poked him in the neck with a piece of salt grass. Preech screamed and slapped his neck, then kicked sand at Rudy when he figured out what was going on.

Oliver sat in a lawn chair as we laid down on a blanket next to the embers from the fire and looked up at the billions of stars. They were so bright I almost had to squint.

"Boys, it's a good idea to figure out the major constellations to help give you an idea of where you are. Those babies helped me get out of some pretty ugly situations during the war."

Rudy pointed to the sky. "Look, there's the Preech Constellation. See his chicken legs, bean pole arms, and absolutely no man parts."

"Ha, ha, very funny musk ox. You're just jealous every insect known to man came to me tonight, probably because I'm so sweet like all the girls at school say."

"I don't know about that, but I'm sure you taste like a donkey. Poor little critters."

Oliver leaned over to get a beer out of the ice chest, and his glasses slid off of his face and into the sand.

Preech picked them up, and blew the sand off before he grabbed a paper towel and poured some water on it. "Mind if I take a look, sir?"

"Give 'em a whirl."

Preech cleaned the glasses, put them on, and looked to the sky. "Holy moley, I can see forever."

He pointed to the moon. "What's that? It's, it's, it's the lunar module. The keys are still in it, and it has a bumper sticker that says, 'How does second place feel, Comrades?'"

Oliver laughed for five minutes straight. Once he caught his breath, Oliver took his glasses back from Preech and pushed himself out of his chair. "Well boys, y'all done great today. I'm gonna hit the sack, so make sure the fire's out before you turn in. Tomorrow, we're going out on a big party boat to go deep sea fishin'."

Rudy saluted him. "Awesome. Thank you, sir. We could use Preech for bait, but I think most fish eat meat, not pansies."

"Not so fast, chowder head. Maybe we can stop on the way so you can take the dive of death to get the bait knife."

Oliver limped to his camper. "Well, y'all figure that out and have a good night."

Curi stopped to lick each of us, then bounded after Oliver and jumped into the camper behind him.

We threw sand over the last of the ashes to make sure the fire was out, then climbed into our sleeping bags.

It felt like I had just closed my eyes when I heard The Oracle making bugle noises outside of the tent. "Up and at 'em boys, it's time to go fishin'."

I jumped right up and wondered why that never happened when I had to get up and go to school.

We drove to the docks again, and this time parked on the far side of the marina. Huge boats as big as whales were tied to the piers.

Oliver whistled as he looked up at the ships. "Those are oil tankers, boys. They fill 'em up in different parts of the world, then bring it over here for us to use."

I felt like the bird in the book *Are You My Mother?* as I stared up at the monster ship. "Can you fish off of it?"

Oliver chuckled. "I cain't see why not. Maybe you and Sir Preech can come up with a way to do it and make a bucket of money."

We followed the signs for the charter boat company and found the one named C'mere Fishy Fishy Fishy and met the captain as we climbed aboard.

Preech saluted him then shook his hand. "Hello Captain. If you see an iceberg, hang a left."

"I think we're pretty safe in the Gulf of Mexico, young man. I will keep an eye out, just in case."

Oliver smiled and shook the captain's hand. "You sure do have a clean vessel here, sir. How far out are we going?"

"About thirty miles. Should be some good snapper fishing on the reefs out there. May hook a tuna or two if we're lucky."

"Ten-four, sir. Lookin' forward to a good time."

"Me too. Enjoy."

The boat was about the size of two school buses tied together, and had fishing rod holders welded along its sides. We found some benches in the front and settled into them. There was a cabin in the center with windows all around it so you could see clear to the other side.

The engines cranked up, and we watched the sun climb over the horizon as we cruised out of the harbor.

Preech looked around. "What happens if someone gets sea sick? Just barf in the water where we're catchin' fish?"

"Yep, I reckon that's what might happen. Hey, do y'all know what the best cure for sea sickness is, boys?"

"Suck on a pickle?" I guessed.

"Nope."

"Look at the horizon?" Preech asked.

"Nope."

Rudy smiled. "Get attacked by a billion mosquitoes so you have something else to think about?"

Oliver laughed. "Well, maybe that would work, but sure would be a bummer out here with nowhere to go but in the shark water. What I've heard is the very best cure for sea sickness is to go sit under a tree."

Preech laughed, and Rudy scratched his head. It took me a few seconds, but I started to laugh when I got it, and laughed harder when Rudy's eyes lit up as he finally got Oliver's joke, too.

Oliver asked me to grab the duffel bag that Rudy had carried onboard. "Okay boys, breakfast of champions."

He unzipped the bag and pulled out a cake wrapped in foil. "I figure this thing has eggs, flour, nuts, and coconut in it. So if your folks ask if we ate good wholesome meals, you won't be far off the mark to say yes."

He broke it into four pieces and set them on paper plates for each of us.

"Kevin, do you mind runnin' inside the cabin and grabbin' a Coke for each of y'all and a cup of coffee for me? I'll get you some money."

119

As he reached for his wallet, I shook my head and stood. "Your money's no good here, sir. I'll get 'em if you make sure these two don't snag my breakfast."

He smiled. "Deal."

I worked my way around the side of the boat and had to grab the handrail to keep from sliding off the side. I wondered how tricky it would be once there was fish blood and guts everywhere from the hundreds of fish we were gonna catch.

I walked into the cabin and noticed that all the tables had a wooden lip on them. I figured it was to keep drinks and food from sliding off when the seas were rough. I ordered our drinks and noticed a huge corkboard filled with pictures.

It was covered with people holding fish, some were as small as bass and others were as big as refrigerators. There was writing on the bottom of the pictures that had the date and the kind of fish. There were some pictures of sharks, but none of them were as big as the one we'd seen. Part of me wanted to catch it and cut it open to get my glove back. The other part of me wanted to get in a shark cage and sit and watch him swim around for a whole day straight.

I thanked the nice lady in the cabin for our drinks and somehow made it back to the front without spilling the coffee and boiling me or one of the other people with it.

"Well, thank you Sir Kevin. Looks like you got good sea legs. I made sure neither one of these rascals got your chow."

Preech and Rudy had finished their cake and stared at mine as they licked their lips.

Oliver took a bottle of Spanish peanuts out of the duffel bag. "Here you go boys. Drink some of your Coke, then put these in it. May sound weird, but they mix real good together."

Rudy and Preech shrugged and pounded half of their Cokes, then used their hand as a funnel and dumped peanuts into the bottles.

I hunkered down over my piece of cake and ate it as fast as I could. "Y'all need to go inside and look at the pictures of fish they caught. There's tons of 'em, and some have crazy names like cobia and skipjack. And there's sharks too, but they looked like the little brother of the one that tried to shred us yesterday."

We passed oil derricks that were taller than any building I'd seen and watched porpoises dive and dance in the water the boat pushed in front of it.

Once we got to the right spot, the deckhands passed out poles and taught us how to use them. The reels were as big as softballs, and the rods were as thick as broomsticks.

Preech whistled and fingered the gizmos on the shiny reel. "You may wanna get one of these for the pond back home, Kev man. Once we get to the island, it may be the only way to land one of the monster catfish."

Another deckhand gave each of us a bag about the size of a pillowcase and handed The Oracle a magic marker.

"You and your grandkids need to write their name on a bag. That a way we'll know where to put the fish, once they catch 'em, in the ice box for y'all to take home."

Oliver grinned and looked at us. "Well grandsons, you reckon you can handle that?"

We grinned back and nodded.

Oliver wrote "Oliver" on his, I wrote "Fish Slayer" on mine, Rudy wrote "#1 Quarterback" on his, and Preech drew a gargantuan hand turkey on his sack.

The deckhand came back, frowned and shook his head when he looked at our bags, and gave us a bucket of bait.

We fished for hours, and all of us caught fish. Mostly red snapper, but Preech caught a drum and Rudy hung a cool brown speckled grouper.

It was late in the afternoon, and the sun baked us on the deck. The captain came on the loudspeaker, and said about another half hour or so and we'd be headin' back.

Preech got up to go to the bathroom, and I stared at the end of my pole, begging a big fish to bite my bait and bend it over. Instead, it was Rudy's pole that bent to the railing, then stopped.

"What a gyp. He must have hung me on the reef."

Rudy pulled with all his might for a few minutes, but it wouldn't budge. He looked at Oliver. "Do you reckon I should cut it loose?"

Oliver was about to answer, when something pulled so hard it ripped Rudy off of the bench and almost yanked him over the side of the boat.

I grabbed the back of his shirt, and Rudy adjusted the drag on the reel. "Whoa, this is a monster fish."

Rudy worked to get the line back in, then blew out a breath of frustration when the line screamed back off of his reel. After a few minutes, most of the other people had stopped fishing to watch Rudy. They stared into the water then back at Rudy as they tried to guess what he had hooked. Through their words I heard a giggle. It was almost girlish, and very familiar. I stood on the bench, looked around, and saw Preech behind the group that had formed to watch Rudy. Preech was biting his fist to try and hold back a laugh, and once he saw me, he waved furiously for me to come with him.

"This is gonna be another good one," I said to myself. I punched Rudy in the shoulder. "Fight 'em good fish slayer. Be back in a few." Then I worked my way through the crowd towards Preech.

CHAPTER 18

Preech half-walked, half-stumbled to the other side of the boat. I saw a group of people as they looked through the windows towards Rudy.

I smiled at Preech. "What'd you do this time?"

He laughed so hard he was out of breath, and hung on to the railing to keep upright. "Well, I was lookin' for a bathroom and saw this guy was tangled up with someone else's line. When I looked at it, I knew it was Rudy's. I saw him triple up on weights earlier, and bingo it was him."

"So did you pull the line really hard to make him think he's got a fish on?"

"No, even better. The guy was going to cut the weights and hook off to go give 'em back, but I gave a deckhand five bucks to tie Rudy's line to that." He pointed to a small machine bolted to the boat deck. It looked like a drill with a soup can attached to the end.

"That machine is used to strip line off of reels super-fast...watch."

The deckhand hit a switch, and it spun like crazy and pulled all of the line off Rudy's reel on the other side of the boat. The crowd cheered and laughed as we looked across the cabin at Rudy. We could see him pulling with all of his might, trying to get the line back onto his reel.

"That is crazy fun. How long you gonna keep him on the hook?"

"I'd do it a week straight if we had time, but I think the captain said we gotta be headin' in soon. Prob'ly five or six more runs and I'll cut him loose."

"Ten-four. I'll boogie back over so he doesn't think anything's up."

I made my way back through the pack of people to my seat in between Rudy and Oliver. Sweat had soaked through Rudy's shirt, and he gritted his teeth as he slowly worked the line onto his reel.

Preech slithered between the crowd and stood next to Rudy. "You reckon that's a boot or somethin'?"

Rudy wiped the sweat off of his forehead with his shirt sleeve and kept his death grip on the pole. "This fish is humongous. It'll prob'ly drop the sea level two feet when I land the sucker."

Preech grinned and patted Rudy on the head. "Good luck with that, Ahab." Then he slid back through the people.

I could barely keep my laughter bottled up, especially when I heard the group from the other side of the boat explode when the gadget ripped the line off of Rudy's reel he worked so hard to capture.

After a few more runs, the line stopped coming in, no matter how hard Rudy pulled. "Dangit, I'm snagged on the reef again."

A minute went by, then the line jerked sideways.

"Hot dog, we're back on."

Rudy furiously reeled the line in, and once it popped out of the water he stared at it in disbelief. There were his three weights, and the smallest sardine I'd ever seen on the tip of his hook.

People slapped Rudy on the back and offered their apologies as they dispersed, and Preech made his way to Rudy's side.

"Bummer dude, that thing is barely as big as a crayon. I think we've got to deduct about two thousand points for you having to work so hard to bring it in."

Rudy scratched his head all the way to the dock.

Once we got back, the deckhands cleaned our fish and packed them in plastic bags.

Preech pointed to the pile of fish heads and guts. "Can we look at the stomachs?"

One of the guys looked at us and shrugged. "Knock yourself out, dudes."

We dug through the entrails and found small headless fish, half-digested squid, and a baby octopus.

"Well boys, about time to load up and get back. Curi's gotta be goin' nuts."

We got back to the campsite, and Curi had dug about halfway to China. All we could see was the tip of his tail and sand flying up out of the hole.

Preech pointed his thumb at Rudy. "Maybe he'll dig it deep enough we can put Bigfoot in there and finally get some peace and quiet...and that horrible stench may even go away."

"What say you boys get another fire goin'. We're gonna really eat like kings with what we caught today," Oliver said, then slipped in the sand and fell to his knees.

I reached down to help him up. "Whoa...you okay, sir?"

Oliver chuckled as he grabbed my forearm and pulled himself up. "Still got a sea leg from the boat trip, I reckon. If you're gonna fall, I guess doin' it on sand is about the best place."

He stood upright, and as we helped him dust the sand off, Rudy whistled and pointed to Oliver's chest. "Hey, is that one of those tags they give you in the army?"

"Y'all ain't seen that before? I wear this thing all the time."

Preech squinted as he bent over to within an inch of it. "Is there a hole in it?"

Oliver held the glistening piece of metal at an angle, so we could look through it. "Yep. What does that hole look like?"

"A heart?" Rudy guessed.

125

Oliver sat back in a lawn chair and peered through the hole at us. "Back in the war, I met the girl of my dreams. Her name was Marlena, and her eyes were bluer than the prettiest ocean water you can imagine. She didn't speak a lick of English, but somehow we knew we were made for each other."

We sat in the sand and made a circle in front of him. I loved it when he talked about the war, and even though this story was about a girl, I hung on every word.

"Me and some of my buddies got caught in a nasty fight one day and barely got out alive. I realized later that a piece of shrapnel had buzzed in and knocked a chunk out of my dog tags. Since it looked like a heart, I took it as a sign and had the chaplain marry us."

Oliver closed his eyes and pinched his lips together. After a couple of minutes, a tear rolled out of his eye and slid down his cheek.

"About a week later, we got into an even nastier battle, and that time I wasn't so lucky."

Everything went dead quiet. I wanted to say something, but I had no idea what.

Oliver put his palm on his forehead like he was trying to hold his skull together. "I woke up state-side and had no idea how I got there. My commanding officer wired me to say that all the soldiers in my squad but me had been wiped out, and the krauts took everyone in Marlena's neighborhood to a concentration camp. I tried for years to track her down, but never heard a peep."

He stood up, and wobbled towards the camper. His shoulders drooped and his voice trailed off as he limped through the thick sand. "In one lousy week I lost my leg, scores of the finest men to walk the planet, and my girl...my wife."

Oliver closed the door to the camper, and Curi whimpered as he looked at it then back at us.

We stared open-mouthed at each other. I'd never seen an adult man cry, much less an army hero like Oliver. I'd always thought cryin' was a sissy thing to do, but since Oliver was the farthest thing ever from a sissy, I figured maybe it was all right to cry every now and then.

Rudy looked at Preech, and his eyes turned to slits. "Smooth move, ex-lax. What'd you go and do that for?"

"What? It was just a question about his dog tag, that's all. I guess we know what happened to his leg now."

I felt like we needed to do something. "Let's get this place ship-shape. Maybe that'll make him feel better."

We threw away trash, even what wasn't ours, and set up things around the campsite that either the wind or Curi had messed up.

After a while Oliver came out of the camper. His eyes were still wet, but his smile was back as he opened a beer and looked at us. "Confucius told me 'he who cuts his own firewood warms himself twice'. What say y'all go find some to chop up and get a fire going so I can fry up the fish we snagged today."

We took off like kangaroo rats into the sand dunes to get the driftwood.

Preech leaned over to grab a big chunk of wood but kicked it before he lifted it to drag back. "Look out for rattlesnakes. I read that they love to hang out in the dunes."

Rudy and I kicked every piece of wood we saw, even if it was as big as a chalkboard eraser. We gathered enough to create a woodpile as big as a bull.

At the campsite, Preech made a small ball of kindling with a paper towel and strips of dry wood and put it under a teepee of twigs like Oliver had taught us. "Does anyone have a match?"

Rudy was in the back of Oliver's truck and poked his head up. "Why yes, my butt and your face."

Oliver choked back a laugh, and Preech shook his fist at Rudy. "Ahh, good one Mr. Commodian. How long you been waitin' to use that?"

Preech knelt back over the fire starter, then shook his head and grinned. "Man, that was a pretty good one...the weak-minded galoot is growing stronger. I gotta step up my game."

Oliver said, "Heads up," and threw Preech a lighter.

Once the fire was roaring, Oliver hooked a pot on the rod across the fire and filled it with oil. "Be sure not to knock this sucker in the fire. It'll make a fireball that would zap every hair off your head."

We watched him cut pieces of the fish into chunks, then roll it in beer batter and drop them into the bubbling hot grease. "You know they're done when they float."

Once the fish were done, Oliver laid them out on a paper plate and covered them with a napkin. "Let's get some tortillas hot and we're ready to eat. Wrap 'em up in a piece of foil and set 'em right next to the fire. Flip 'em around every now and then 'till they're hot."

We helped Oliver finish cooking, then sat in our lawn chairs and ate like a pack of wolves. Oliver threw balls of beer batter he had fried to Curi. "These are called hush puppies. Someone told me they were invented to give to dogs to keep 'em from yappin' while you cooked, so they named 'em hush puppies."

On the last day at the beach, Oliver woke us with his bugle noises like he had every morning. "Rise and shine, Troopers. Once y'all break down everything and pack it up, criss-cross the area to get the trash and make sure all we leave is footprints."

"Sir, yes sir," we said.

As we climbed out of the tent, Oliver pointed to some pieces of broken beer bottles. "Please make sure you pick up them hippy shells as well. Let's make sure the folks behind us have a nice, clean piece of beach to enjoy."

We covered the entire campsite and picked up every last piece of paper or glass we found.

Oliver checked the ropes holding everything in the bed of the truck, then looked around the campsite and nodded his approval. "Load up boys, we're headin' back. I appreciate all of the help."

As we climbed into the truck I shrugged and looked at The Oracle. "Sorry we didn't achieve our pirate treasure mission. I hope you weren't countin' on the gold to buy somethin' with."

Oliver chuckled as he slammed the truck door and started the engine. "Maybe that mission wasn't complete, but if laughin' and havin' a good time were it, I think we set a world record."

After we drove for a few hours, Oliver decided it was time to gas up. As he pulled to a stop by the pumps, Rudy reached under the seat and grabbed a tire tool. "I'll check the perimeter, sir."

He jumped out of the truck and took off around the side of the building. Oliver grinned and watched him disappear around the corner. "You know, that deal that happened in Louisiana was a once in a million thing, but it feels good to know y'all got my back in case it ever happens again."

Preech and I climbed out of the truck and stretched. "We're gonna grab some Cokes and snacks. Can we get you anything?"

"How 'bout a time machine to get us back in a few seconds instead of two days of drivin'?"

Preech's eyes lit up. "I'm workin' on one, actually. I still got a lot of work to do, but should be done in a year or so once I find the parts I need."

Oliver patted him on the back. "Well, maybe it'll make the trip seem faster knowin' you'll have one done down the road."

Rudy came around the far side of the building and I waved to him. Rudy tapped his forehead with a salute and yelled, "Perimeter secured, sir. Permission to buy something that will rot my teeth?"

Oliver saluted him back and answered, "Permission granted."

Preech and I walked together to the store. As we got to a window, he skidded to a stop to look at his reflection. "Okay, exactly how long have I had a magic marker moustache?"

I couldn't hold back a laugh. "Well, it started about the time you took a nap on the boat on our way back from fishin'. And I think someone refreshed it last night."

Preech licked his finger and tried to rub the black ink off of his face. "Ahhh, now it makes sense. I wondered why everyone was smilin' so much on the boat ride. I thought they were just nice fishin' folk, but now I know it was the work of the brainless wonder."

Rudy was standing just inside the window and did a little finger wave before he laughed and clasped his hands over his head in triumph.

Preech smirked and returned the finger wave. "Well, they say to keep your friends close and enemies even closer. I had a prank hit me in a dream last night that's gonna rock his world."

CHAPTER 19

The last days of summer disappeared like spit on a griddle, and we became seventh graders. It was the first day of school, and within ten minutes, Preech, Rudy, and I were called to Coach Stark's office. Going to the principal's office is one thing, but being called to the coach's office terrified me even more.

Rudy strutted down the dark hall that led to the coach's office. "We're gonna own these halls this year fellas. I can feel it."

Preech crinkled his nose. "Nobody's been in here all summer, and it still smells like a moldy jock strap. Why did Coach call for us? Do you think we're in trouble or somethin'?"

Rudy laughed. "No way, man. I figure he wants to know what size trophy will fit in our trophy cases at home. There's a trophy for every player on the team that gets first place for District. I think second place gets a ribbon or something, and everyone else just goes home to cry themselves to sleep."

I wish I could be as sure about things as Rudy, but something told me football wasn't gonna work for me no matter how hard I tried. "Umm, do you think he needs a manager too? Tryouts the other day didn't go so good for me."

Rudy put his arm around me. "Don't worry, Kev man. We're a package deal. If you don't make the team, I'm gonna tell Coach he should find a new quarterback."

It felt awesome that Rudy was such a good buddy that he'd give up his dream to help me out. I cringed when I realized that I still hadn't done anything to help with his Ted problem. I swore to myself that the sun would not rise again without me putting a plan together.

Light poured from the slightly-cracked door to the coach's office, and Preech dropped his voice to a whisper. "Dudes, did y'all see how Coach Stark got even bigger over the summer? I think his muscles even have muscles."

Rudy nodded and whispered back. "I heard he drinks a dozen raw eggs for breakfast and eats nothing but meat all day long. They say you can crack an egg anywhere on him, and I believe it."

I gagged at the thought of him slurping down raw eggs, and a fresh wave of panic crept into my chest. What if he wanted us to do a chin up competition, and the loser had to make raw egg-shakes for him for the rest of the year? I would barf every time.

As we walked in, Coach Stark's voice boomed off of the walls and almost pushed me backwards. "Hey boys, how y'all doin'? You had a mighty fine tryout the other day Rudy. I think you're gonna put us on the map this year. I knew there was somethin' special about you when we met at the end of the school year last spring."

Coach was sitting behind a normal-sized desk, but he was so big it looked like one from Milly's class. He swiveled his body to look at Preech. "And you are Preech, right? You had some great catches. Did y'all spend some time together workin' on football this summer?"

Preech smiled. "Yessir, we did. My Uncle Oliver let us play on his pasture. We got most of the team out a bunch of times."

He nodded, then turned his head toward me. His AstroTurf-green eyes looked right through me. "And you're Kelvin, right? Sorry about that kid, maybe next year."

Rudy cleared his throat. "Sorry about what, sir? Kevin might have missed a couple of balls, but he just hasn't found his rhythm yet."

132

"Sorry guys, but the roster is full. We used up all the uniforms on kids that can actually play football."

I could feel my face turn as red as a baboon's butt. There had to be a nicer way to say that.

Rudy gritted his teeth. "Coach, sir, you gotta let Kevin play. It just won't be the same without him."

"Well, that's the way it is. I'm the coach, and I made my decision."

Rudy shook his head. "Okay, okay. But you did say we ran out of uniforms. If we could find one more, can Kevin be on the team?"

Coach Stark rubbed his chin for a few seconds. "I really don't think we got any more uniforms, but if we had one more I reckon we'd let him on. Just don't get your hopes up, because we can't afford to buy any more."

Rudy winked at me. "All right, great. Is that what you called us for?"

"Nope, actually I need something done fast and done right. I asked Principal Mackenzie who could make something happen for me, and he mentioned you three."

Preech popped his knuckles. "Who do want whacked, and where do you want us to put the body?"

Coach Stark laughed and took out a pen and paper. "Well, nothin' like that. Since y'all are in the same Ag class, I talked to your teacher and he gave me the green light on y'all makin' a new paddle for me. The one I had at my last school somehow disappeared."

Preech gulped as Coach drew a paddle and measurements on the paper. "That's gonna be as long as a baseball bat!"

"Yep, with a wood cover, a solid steel core, and holes drilled through it. I want that sucker to whistle when I swing it. Also, y'all make a sign that says Don't Let Your Procrastination Become My Chaos so I can hang it over the paddle on the wall in my classroom."

Rudy's eyes bugged out a little when he looked at the finished drawing on coach's desk. "Is that how your other one looked?"

"Yep, pretty much. The thing is, I never had to use it...imagine that."

They started talking about metals, wood types, and other stuff. I tried to focus, but my mind drifted to things like football and fishing. Did I really want to play football, or did Rudy want me play because we were buddies and that was his thing? More importantly, did Rudy like to fish as much as I did, or did he go fishing because *I* liked it so much?

I wondered if part of becoming a man was learning how to figure out the difference, then doing the right thing.

Preech patted my back and I snapped out of it. "Will do, Coach, we'll get right on it."

Rudy raised his hand and pointed to a door on the far side of the office. "Would it be okay if we looked around in there?"

Coach Stark opened a file on his desk and waved us away with his hand. "Sure, fine, but make sure you get to Ag class on time to get started on makin' 'The Whistler' for me."

Rudy turned the handle, and the rusty old steel door groaned as he put his shoulder against it and forced it open.

Preech pinched his nose shut. "Holy cow, this could be the epicenter of the stench. It smells like the stuff my uncle uses at his funeral home, but nastier. Let's get out of here."

Rudy pulled the top of his tee shirt over his nose. "Not so fast. One of the guys on the varsity team said a kid locked himself in here after a seventh grade football game a few years ago."

I sucked some air in my mouth and sounded like a frog as I tried to hold the breath in as I talked. "What's the big deal about that?"

"The kid missed a last-second field goal in the only game they would've won all season. It crushed him so bad, they say he locked himself in here for hours. The coaches were gonna take the door off the hinges to get him out, but he came runnin' out naked as a jaybird and never played football again."

Preech shook his head. "I can smell why."

Rudy pointed his thumb at me as he stepped over the piles of wadded up junk. "If he ran out of here with nothin' on, you reckon there might be a uniform somewhere for Kev?"

Preech's eyebrows shot up. "Ohh, gotcha. Y'all want some gum? To stick up your nose maybe?"

Rudy and I nodded, and the three of us folded over pieces of Juicy Fruit and stuck them up our noses. I couldn't smell it anymore, but the air was so thick and funky I could still taste it. I looked at the shelves of dust-covered cleaning supplies and thought that Ben Franklin himself had probably set them there and they hadn't been touched since.

Preech stretched his leg out to touch a pile of rags with the tip of his tennis shoe. "You know guys, rats are too proud to live here. I think we should—"

Rudy interrupted him. "Jackpot baby, look right there."

Through the dim light, we saw a piece of red cloth under a stack of broken broomsticks. Rudy took one of the broomsticks, snagged part of the material, and pulled it from the pile. It was a real jersey, with a bright silver number '83' that shined through the dusty air.

Rudy held it above his head like an Olympian holds a gold medal. "How awesome, it's even got a receiver number on it."

Rudy threw it to me, and I wished I could be as happy as he was. "Thanks my man. I'll take it home, and maybe my mom can wash it a couple of hundred times to get the smell out."

Preech made a circle sign with his finger. "Let's bug out. There's no tellin' how many years we're shavin' off our lives breathin' this stuff."

We made our way out of the dank room and sucked in clean air when we got back to Coach Stark's office. I helped Rudy pull the door closed, then he turned triumphantly to the coach and pointed at the jersey. "Voila, one football jersey."

Coach looked up from his desk and did a small nod. As he did, he flicked his finger at me. "Well, I'm a man of my word. Whatshisname is on the roster. I think there's a set of mangled shoulder pads and a slightly cracked helmet around here somewhere. And, the last pair of pants is a little pinkish, but better than nothin'."

I wanted to ask what "mangled," "slightly cracked," and "pinkish" meant, but Rudy grabbed my elbow and led me to the door. "Thanks Coach, you won't be sorry. We gotta boogie to get to work on your project. See you at practice."

With that we took off down the hall, and when the warning bell rang, we sprinted full speed to make it to the Ag barn in time for class.

CHAPTER 20

The first game was about to start, and Coach Stark pulled me into his office. "Okay, Casey, it's almost go time. I know Rudy is your best buddy or whatever, so how's he feelin'?"

I wanted to correct him about my name, but the last million times didn't work so I decided to let it pass. "Well, he ate three hamburgers at lunch but skipped the fries so the grease wouldn't slow him down. And he told me to tell the janitor to put extra Kleenex in the visitor's locker room, because he said there's gonna be a lot of cryin' in there after the game."

Coach smiled. "Awesome. And you never know, if we get way, way, ahead, you may even see the field. But no promises, okay Kenny?"

I nodded and left the coach in his office. We ran out of the locker room, warmed up, then huddled under the goal post for the cheerleaders to unfold a big paper banner for us to run through.

When Coach yelled for us to go, Rudy was at the front of the group and held his palms out for everyone to stop. His head bobbed over the rest of the team as he jumped up and down, and when he saw me, he waved for me to come to the front.

I ran around the others players and stopped between Rudy and Preech.

Rudy took his mouthpiece out. "This is what it's all about, Kev."

Preech smiled and slapped my helmet. "I already got a spot cleaned off of my desk at home for the trophy we'll get at the end of the season. You ready?"

I nodded. Then we ran though the banner with the rest of the team. I said a quick prayer of thanks the paper didn't tackle me and cause me to trip and wipe out the whole team.

I looked at the stands, and counted about thirty people. As we reached the sideline, I spotted my parents, Preech's parents, and Daisy. Oliver was sitting next to her and used his cane to beat the stands like a drum.

Rudy got ready to go out for the coin toss and I realized I'd never seen him look so happy. He turned his head slowly to soak in everything as he clenched and unclenched his fists. I wondered if I looked like that when we were at the pond, or staring at the ocean when I had a hook in the water.

We won the toss, and chose to accept the kick. Our returner made it to the thirty yard line, and Rudy slapped Coach Stark on the back as he ran on the field. I watched the coach call in a pass play, but everyone was shocked by what happened.

Rudy shook his head 'no', then lined up and Rudy took the snap. It was a quarterback keeper, and Rudy took off through everyone.

Coach Stark screamed and waved his arms in circles. "What are you doing? Go around them, around them."

Rudy looked like a one-man wrecking ball as he plowed over every person on the other team. He even slowed down to knock over a defender who had half-heartedly chased him to the end zone.

The crowd erupted when Rudy crossed the goal line, then Coach erupted when Rudy made it back to the sideline. "What the heck were you doin'? Great run and all, but dangit boy you need to run around the other guys, not into them. And another thing, you run the play I call. You got that?"

Rudy spit his mouthpiece out and howled like a werewolf. "Got it, Coach."

Coach Stark grunted his approval. "You gonna be able to keep that pace up for a whole game?"

"No problem, sir." Then Rudy pointed to the sky. "You see, the thing is my real dad's watchin'. I wanna make him proud."

For the first time ever, the coach was speechless. He blinked a couple of times, nodded, then left to yell at everyone else.

The game went by like a blur, and the coolest part of the blur was Rudy. He got a little better at running around the other guys, but if they were anywhere close, Rudy still put a lick on them. He later told me that he'd picture Ted behind every other guy's facemask, and it gave him a kick to plow 'em over.

I kicked myself for not doing a dang thing to help him with Ted yet.

We blasted through each team we played and got better every week.

It was the last game before the district championship, and once again it was the "Rudy Show." It was awesome to watch him run so fast—it looked like everyone on the other team was standing still.

With three minutes left, we were ahead by four touchdowns, and I was in my usual spot next to Coach Stark. Since I never got to play, I figured I'd hang out close to him to see what play he called. It was cool to watch the play as it went from his clipboard to real-life on the field.

I looked up at Rudy, and almost didn't catch the signal. He looked frustrated, like he'd been doing it a while. It was the finger-on the chin drum roll that Curly from the The Three Stooges did, and it meant that the "Kevin Shuffle" was on.

I dropped my helmet, then picked it up and tried to buckle the chinstrap as I put it on. I'd done it a lot of times, but for some reason it felt like my fingers were made of rubber and wouldn't work.

Just like we planned at Oliver's farm, Rudy was about to hike the ball when Jeff Jones, our running back, faked like he was hurt and fell down. He grabbed his ankle, and rolled back and forth on the grass turf.

Coach cursed and called a time out, then looked around as the manager ran on the field to help Jeff. I stood in front of him with my helmet on, and when he noticed, Coach frowned and slammed his hand on my shoulder pads. "I reckon you get some playin' time after all, Kent. I called in a run for the other back, so don't screw anything up."

I ran to the huddle, and Preech and Rudy grinned so big their mouthpieces almost slid out of their mouths.

Rudy cleared his throat. "Okay guys, it's the 'Kevin Shuffle,' just like we practiced at Oliver's, on three. Ready, break."

The rest of the team yelled 'break', and it sounded ten thousand times louder than it did when I stood next to Coach Stark.

I lined up where I thought I should, but Rudy got under the center, looked at me, and shook his head. He backed up and pulled me to the left about four feet, nodded, then got back under center.

I saw the ball get hiked and Rudy gave it to me, then I entered a total dream world. I took off for the sideline like we'd practiced, then turned at the last second and ran towards the end zone. It felt like I was running in quicksand as I watched the wall of blockers form next to me.

The play was something Oliver worked on with us, and he said it had football genius and unpredictable "scorched earth" mixed in to confuse the enemy.

Every player started the play by blocking someone for a second or two, then ran to the sideline to form a protective wall. I ran as fast as I could, but everyone else seemed to jog to keep in step with me.

Rudy was the first blocker I saw. He slapped me on the butt pad and yelled, "Move it gramma, we ain't got all day," before he peeled off to knock out a linebacker.

Preech was the next blocker I saw run up beside me, and he did a quick prayer thing with his fingers on his heart and head before he jumped backwards into the arms of two defenders. He knocked them down, and it seemed like a couple more defenders fell in the tangled blur of uniforms that quickly disappeared behind me.

I almost tripped on my own shoelaces twice, but I made it to the end zone with a couple of my teammates running backwards to protect me.

It was so awesome I pumped my fists in the air and let out a scream. Preech and Rudy got to me first and jumped around before they picked me up and put me on their shoulders. We started to sing *We are the Champions* by Queen, something we always sang at the top of our lungs when it played on the radio.

The celebration stopped when Coach Stark stomped onto the field and threw his clipboard down in front of us. "What was that?!"

I slid back to the grass with a thump.

Spit flew from the coach's mouth as he barked at Rudy. "What the heck were you thinkin'? My number one player throwing blocks in the fourth quarter of a game that's almost over!"

Then Coach Stark grabbed Preech's facemask and pulled it within an inch of his face. "My number one receiver doing the same thing, but looking more like a drunk circus chimp jumping around like that!" screamed Coach. "If I ever see you leave your feet to block again I'll make it where you can't jump for a long, long, time."

He let go of Preech's facemask and swiveled his head towards me. My spine tingled as Coach Stark's crazy green eyes bored into my brain. "And my number one, umm, number one, uhh, bench warmer I guess."

Coach had a brutal way of getting to the point.

"We gotta work on your speed, boy. I could have built two houses with my bare hands in the time it took you to run sixty yards."

Coach Stark took a deep breath and had a hint of a smile but was still grinding his teeth. The veins in his neck and on his forehead started to shrink back to normal.

He shook his head and said, "Well, I think I know why y'all did this, and even though it was for a buddy, it don't make it right. I will say that tonight y'all burned your one and only get-out-of-jail-free card. If you ever try a stunt like this again, I will not only run you till you puke, I will keep running you to till your legs fall out of their sockets."

After a brief pause, Coach growled, "Am I clear?"

"Okay, Coach, I hear you," said Rudy as he looked down at his cleats.

I gulped and nodded, "Yes, sir."

"I've never been more clear on anything in my whole life, Coach Stark," answered Preech.

We waited for Coach to pick up his clipboard and walk away, then smiled and high-fived each other. Rudy picked up the football and gave it to me, and he and Preech bumped me back and forth between them as we walked to the sideline.

I was happy to have scored a touchdown, and even happier that Rudy and Preech helped out and didn't get hurt. I had hoped my first score would have made me feel more manly. Outside of sweat squirting out of every part of my body, it didn't change a thing.

The day before the District Championship, Rudy and I ate our lunches and looked over the plays Coach Stark had given him to study for the game.

He took a pencil and changed a route from a fly to a curl, then smiled and nodded. "The 'Cats aren't gonna know what hit 'em. Have you picked out a spot for your trophy yet?"

"I think it'll fit on the desk in my room. You feelin' good about the game?"

Rudy snorted and wadded his brown paper lunch bag into a ball. "Dude, they're gonna be cryin' for mercy by half time." He got up and tossed the sack into a trash can. "Gotta run. Coach wanted to go over some other stuff with me."

As he got up, Preech walked in and grinned at Rudy. "Hola, numbskull. I thought I smelled you in here."

Rudy smiled back at him. "Is it zoo day, or did they let weasels eat with people today?"

"Ha, good one. By the way, Nurse Gillespie is lookin' for you. Maybe she got some word on a brain transplant, or maybe she's got the hots for you."

Rudy gulped and looked around. "Man, she's been after me for weeks. She's like two-hundred years old, and I don't know what the deal is...it's creepy."

I knew exactly what the deal was and had to pinch my leg through my jeans to keep from laughing.

Rudy eased his head out in the hall, then jumped back into the cafeteria. He spied the door that led outside, then ran through it and took off.

Nurse Gillespie walked in and looked around, and I could tell she was disappointed when she didn't see Rudy. Her eyes lit up when she saw us. "Hello, sweet boys...have you seen your friend Rudy around?"

I pinched myself harder to keep a straight face. "Yes ma'am, I believe Coach Stark needed him for something. Is there anything we can help you with?"

She looked at us for a few seconds, then shook her head. "No, thank you. I just really need some time with him. Please instruct him to come see me."

"Yes ma'am, will do." I said, then bit my tongue as hard as I could to try and stop the laugh that was about to blow my head off.

She turned back into the hall, and Preech laughed so hard milk squirted out of his nose. "Man, that was close. Two more seconds and I would have lost it."

I grinned and rubbed my leg. "I know, I know. I pinched my leg so hard I think it's bleeding. Did you drop off another letter?"

"Yep, and I have to say it's my personal favorite. I've dropped one every week or so, and today's was the last one I'm gonna do. I've got copies of all of them. Do you wanna see 'em before I destroy the evidence?"

"Oh heck yeah. But let's go to the playground so we can eat 'em if we see someone coming."

We walked out of the cafeteria to the farthest edge of the playground and stopped next to the shed that had lawnmowers and stuff piled in it.

Preech pulled a crumpled pile of papers from his pocket, then shuffled them around to put them in order. "It took me a while to teach myself to write exactly like the meathead, but I think I nailed it. I came up with the first one during our trip to Florida, then the rest flowed like volcano magma."

Dear Doctor Gillespie,

Teddy Roosevelt came to me in a dream last night. We shared high tea, and he showed me a design for the perfect meat helmet. After a lot of trial and error, I have found that wearing ladies' undergarments is the only thing that shuts the pie holes of the screaming voices in my head.

If you have time I really think I need to talk with you.

Ciao,

Rudy

I laughed, and Preech handed me the next one.

My Dear Betta,

The women's underwear is still doing the trick. I tried silks, but they made me feel as though I had wet myself. Cottons and woolens are my favorites, with homemade burlap on Fridays. What's your preference? With the voices in my head diminished, I can clearly hear the animals speaking to me again. The squirrels are the only creatures that have yet to assimilate to my plan of world dominance. I shall deal with them swiftly and justly if the insolent attitude continues.

I hope you can find time in your busy schedule to discuss.

By the way, have you tried the tuna loaf in the cafeteria? DELICIOUS!!

Hasta Lambrusco,

Rudy

I laughed harder, and Preech wiped his face with his shirt sleeve as he handed me the next letter.

To Whom it May Concern,

After repeated attempts to get time with you, I have realized my affairs are either of no interest to you or out of your scope of expertise. If I am incorrect, please give me a few precious seconds the next time you can scrape them together. I assure you Dr. Marcus Welby would never treat his patients like this.

By the way, the burgundy shawl you wore the other day was absolutely stunning.

That guy named Rudy

Preech smiled and bowed as he gave the last letter. "Okay, here's my favorite. I just took his biography from the ones we had to do for English class and put 'according to the prophecy' after every sentence."

My name is Rudy, according to the prophecy.

I was born in Pennsylvania, according to the prophecy.

I live on Elm Street, according to the prophecy.

My mom is named Daisy and stepdad is Ted, according to the prophecy.

I have a fish named Gilbert, according to the prophecy.

I almost saw my best friends get eaten by a shark, according to the prophecy.

I hope to be an army soldier or pro football player someday, according to the prophecy.

Love, Rudy, according to the prophecy

CHAPTER 21

I gave Preech a high five. "Man, that's crazy funny. You reckon we should get rid of 'em?"

Preech crumpled a couple of the sheets and tore them into tiny pieces. "Yeah, let's make these as small as possible, then I'll put 'em in the burn pile at home."

Once the pieces were as small as ants, Preech nodded and poured them into his pocket. "Hey, big game tomorrow. Did Rudy tell you about the new plays?"

"Yep...looks like some great ones." We walked towards the school, and I asked, "How you feelin' about the game?"

Preech took a deep breath, then blew it out and looked at me. "You know the feelin' when you lean back in a chair and catch yourself at the last second?"

"Yeah."

Preech shrugged. "I feel like that all the time, dude. This game is huge."

"You know, once I asked The Oracle if he was scared during the war."

"You did? I betcha he said never, ever... right?"

"Nope, the exact opposite. He told me he was scared about every second of every minute of every hour he was there. He said sometimes fear is a part of life, but what you do or don't do is what matters."

Preech rubbed his chin. "Well then, you reckon I should let it fuel me to prank Rudy? If I get ahold of his Greek mythology book, I'm thinkin' of changin' some of the names to things like 'Testiclees' to see if he says something during class."

I shook my head and snickered. "If that does the trick for you, go for it, I reckon. What do you think he'll do when he finds out about the Nurse Gillespie project?"

Preech smiled. "Ohh, I think he'll be angry, like King Kong when the planes were shootin' at him. But then he'll return fire, and I gotta say, that pinhead has come up with some pretty good ones lately. He's one tenacious monkey, and quite the worthy adversary."

"Yeah," I said, "You know, I've been thinkin' about what I can do to help Rudy with Ted, but I got nothin'. Ted's comin' off the rig soon, and I just hope it's after the game. I don't think he'd come to the game anyway, but if he did, that prob'ly won't help Rudy."

"Yep, you're right. Let's say we get the game behind us, then you and I can figure out somethin' to do. Maybe even call in reinforcements, like Coach Stark and the army or somethin'."

A wave of relief washed over me. "Dude, that would be awesome."

The day for the big game came, and I could taste the excitement in the air.

Rudy stopped me in the hall. "You know what I heard? There's gonna be a reporter for the paper at the game today. Will you act like my agent and say there's a charge for takin' pictures of the champs?"

I smiled back at him and wished I had a tenth of his courage. "Heck yeah, and I'll tell him that the pros are callin', and he needs to buy stock in Wheaties because they want to put you on the next box."

He slugged my shoulder and took off. I walked down the hall, and for the first time since I could remember, I felt really good. Maybe it was because we were actually going to make a plan to help Rudy with Ted, or maybe it was because we were hours away from being county champions.

By half-time, the feeling was gone. Maybe because we were two touchdowns behind, or maybe it was because Coach Stark screamed so loud his spit hit us like he was a water sprinkler.

"Rudy, what the heck's the deal? It's like those guys know everything we're gonna do, and are two steps ahead."

"I know, I know. It's like they've been watchin' us or somethin'."

Coach was chewing his metal whistle so hard I thought it was going to pinch shut. He frowned and looked at Rudy. "This is your team, and y'all are better than this. What say you try that 'hobo crawl' play you did with Courtney there."

Rudy's eyes turned to slits. "His name is Kevin, Coach, and he's done everything you've asked him, plus some. Kevin's got more heart in his pinky than you or most of the guys on this team."

I sucked air through my teeth and braced myself as I waited for the coach to explode.

Instead, he smiled and smacked his forehead with his palm. "That's it...if they've been watching us, I doubt they saw the last plays of a game that was done by the third quarter."

Rudy looked up at Coach Stark. "So..."

Coach grabbed Rudy by the shoulder pads and pulled him off of the locker room bench. "We run that play, but you are the hotshot." Then he pointed at Preech. "Forget what I told you before. You block any way you want. Break some teeth if you have to. I don't care if they're your teeth or the other guy's."

Coach ran to the chalkboard and drew it up, then quickly drew up five other plays. "Y'all got five minutes to learn these. Make it snappy."

We got the ball on the kickoff, and Rudy scored on the first run of the "Kevin Shuffle." Coach let Rudy play defense, and on the next drive he intercepted a ball and ran it back for a touchdown. Rudy ran for another score late in the fourth quarter, and we won our first ever District Championship.

The crowd exploded. The band played *We Will Rock You*, or maybe it was *The Star-Spangled Banner*, but either way it was one of the coolest things ever.

Daisy hugged Rudy as she found him in the crowd, and Oliver patted him on the shoulder pads. Coach Stark appeared next to Rudy. "This is one heck of a boy you got here, ma'am."

She smiled and nodded. "Yes he is. I am blessed."

Coach looked at Rudy. "You might want to buy him a new pair of shoes. He had quite the half-time speech, and those will come in handy real soon."

Rudy gulped and shrugged. "Well, it worked, right?"

"We'll see," smiled Coach as he left to celebrate with the rest of the team.

CHAPTER 22

Preech and I stood in my front yard and looked at the diagram he had drawn. I smiled and slapped him on the back. "That is the best invention ever, dude. We'll be able to fish the island and use it next time we go to the coast with Oliver."

Preech nodded and pointed to the paper. "Yep, the cage on top will keep snakes from attacking from the trees, and the sides have pointed sticks that will keep them from coming out of the water and gettin' us. And all three of us will fit on it, but we may need a trailer to pull it around."

"Awesome, man."

Rudy rode up on his bike and slid to a stop on the grass.

Preech shook his head and waved his hand at the freshly-raked yard. "Well, well, just like a blister. Show up when all the work's done."

I started to laugh, but stopped when I saw Rudy's black eye. "Whoa, you okay man?"

Rudy shook his head, and I could tell he was doing his best to keep from crying. "Uhhh fellas, I need your help. Like today—like right now."

I could feel my dream of fishing the island slip away like trying to hold water in my hand.

"You know, it's great fishing weather, and Preech figured out how to get us to the island. Can what you need wait until tomorrow?"

Rudy's lips trembled. "I almost did it on my own, but chickened out. There's no way I'd go to the Flats by myself, and I really need y'all to go. Please."

Preech's threw his hands in the air. "Dude, our parents will hammer us if we go to the Flats...if we even lived to talk about it."

The milk that had been so good and cold on my Frosted Flakes breakfast curdled in my stomach. "Yeah, buddy, I've heard cops don't even go in there."

Rudy bit his bottom lip and talked out of the side of his mouth. "I wish there was some other way. Ted went way too far, and it has to end. Today."

I watched Preech slowly nod his agreement as he stared back and forth from Rudy's black eye to the grass.

"Okay, we'll go. Let me grab somethin' real quick."

Rudy patted my back. "Man, thanks so much. Make it quick, we gotta be there in an hour."

I ran into my room and dug through my underwear drawer until I found the switchblades I'd snuck back from Mexico in my boot. I put them in one pocket, then grabbed an iron cross off the wall and crammed it into my other pocket.

On the way out of my room I looked back and my eyes stopped on the District Championship trophy that sat on my desk.

I wondered if I'd ever see it again.

My mom stopped me in the hall by the front door and put her palm on my forehead. "Hey hon, you look kinda pale. You feelin' all right?"

"Nope, I'm good," I lied and gave her a hug. It killed me to not tell her what was up, but I knew she'd blow her lid and stop us from going. Oliver had always told us to "Do the next right thing." Even though it was a perfect fishing day and we had a way to get to the island, it felt like helping Rudy was the next right thing to do.

I threw the front door open and jumped down the steps as I hollered back at her. "Chores are done. I'll be back before dinner."

Rudy and Preech were stopped at the end of the street, and I hopped on my bike and didn't look back as I pedaled to them.

They were wide-eyed and quiet, and we rode in silence to the main road that led out of town.

As we cruised by my church, I noticed the pastor's car was there. Sure, he'd caught me playing poker during Bible study once, and he saw me accidentally smash a window of the house next to the church with a softball, but where was he now to stop us and talk us out of going?

I looked at the tombstones in the small grassy area next to the church and hoped they'd get a cool one with a fish on it for me if the trip to the Flats was my last bike ride ever.

I felt the knives click together in my pocket, and even though I never figured out how to work them, I hoped they wouldn't open in my pocket and stab me.

Preech broke the silence. "Ummm, what are we gonna do once we get there?"

Rudy squinted at Preech's watch. "Well, should be a quick in and out. In exactly forty minutes, I'm gonna meet a guy behind a bar they call Larry's. Once I pay him, I'll have what I need to take care of Ted forever."

A million questions screamed through my head, but my mouth and throat were so dry I couldn't make a sound. It tasted like I'd swallowed fifty cotton balls and drank a gallon of sand to chase them down.

As we pedaled out of town towards our doom, I thought of wiping out and faking I'd hurt myself. They'd seen me wipe out a thousand times, and I was pretty sure I could pull off a doozy. Then I thought about all the cool things Rudy had done for me, and I couldn't think of one measly thing I'd done to help him. So I kept pedaling.

Rudy waved his hand to stop us when we got to the train tracks. Once we crossed them, the Flats were about four football fields away. The houses looked like a sad bunch of grapes dying on a vine, and a few small buildings in the middle slumped like drunk monkeys.

"Thanks so much for coming guys. I will never forget—" Rudy's speech was interrupted by the quick burst of a police siren, which made us jump a foot off of our bike seats.

I looked back to see two policemen in a squad car, and the relief that washed over me almost made me cry.

The driver got out and shook his head as he approached us. "Boys, I truly hope y'all are about to turn around and high-tail it home. That ain't no place for y'all."

Rudy puffed his chest out. "Well, I just gotta go see someone about somethin'. Is that against the law?"

I noticed the shiny name tag on the officer's uniform which said "Officer Duncan." "Well, smart mouth, that ain't against the law. But I sure do wish stupidity was, 'cause that'd make my job a whole lot easier."

The other officer was out of the car and stood behind me. He laughed and slapped the gun in his holster. "Good one, Jeff. I gotta write that down." His name tag said "Officer Shipley."

Officer Duncan craned his neck to get a good look at Rudy. "Hey, I know you, boy. We've been called out to your house a couple of times when your daddy got too rowdy. And how'd you get that shiner? Been fightin'?"

Rudy gritted his teeth. "He's my stepdad. Not my daddy. We gotta go." With that, Rudy pedaled down the slope of the train tracks towards the Flats.

Preech and I shrugged at the officers and followed Rudy, and my heart sank to the balls of my feet.

Once we got closer, the smell of trash, burning rubber, and some kind of cooking meat filled the air.

The first thing we saw was a man who was so old his skin looked paper-thin, brown and wrinkled like a leaf. He stared at us as he sat on the curb, and his voice sounded like two bricks rubbing together. "Hey boys, what cha'll doin' here? You got any money?"

Rudy cleared his throat. "Hello sir, we're here on business. Can you kindly point me to Larry's?"

The old man made a sound more like a bark than a laugh and pointed down the street. "It ain't hard to find. Just head down there and take a left at the second street and you'll see it. I don't go in that deep unless I have to. You got protection?" He said as he made a gun with his thumb and finger.

"Yes sir, brought my posse."

When the man realized it was me and Preech, he started to laugh so hard that it turned into a nasty, raspy cough. I was scared one of his lungs was going to pop out. We nodded our thanks and eased our bikes down the dusty street. We rode so close to each other our pedals almost rubbed together.

We followed the directions and found Larry's. The parking lot glittered with so many shards of broken bottles I could barely see the asphalt. Oliver would have totally disapproved of the millions of "hippie shells" that littered the parking lot.

Rudy grabbed my elbow. "Okay, I said I'd be by myself. Y'all just hang out while I go behind the store and get what I gotta get, then we're outta here."

I slapped him on the back, then watched him disappear around the back of the store. It felt like the protective shield that got us so deep into the Flats disappeared as Rudy pedaled away.

We got off our bikes, and the glares from the guys that sat in front of the store made the hair on the back of my neck prickle.

Preech leaned over and whispered, "What the heck is he doin'?"

"I dunno. He said we'd be outta here quick...I hope."

A long car pulled within inches of us, and the dark driver's side window rolled down. The smell of weird smoke poured out and almost knocked me over.

The driver was as big as a grizzly bear. "Well, well, well, what do we have here? The man's teeth were black and rotted, and the sour smell of his breath almost made me barf. "It appears y'all didn't pay the toll to get into my world. Them bikes should do for a start, but it's gonna take a lot more to ever see your mama and daddy again."

The back door opened and two guys jumped out and shoved us. Then they picked up our bikes and stuffed them in the trunk.

For some reason Preech started to scream scriptures at the top of his lungs, which angered the driver. I'd never heard Preech make such a weird sound.

The man snapped his fingers to make Preech stop. "What you got in your pockets? Any money?"

I reached into my pocket and was shocked when I pulled my hand out and saw the switchblades. Preech's eyes almost bugged out of their sockets, and his hand shook as I gave him one.

The man in the car sneered and let out a deep, evil laugh. "You never bring a knife to a gunfight, stupid boy." His cold eyes reminded me of the shark that almost shredded us.

He looked towards the back seat and said, "Do it."

I glanced at Preech and saw he was trying to figure out how to open the knife. When I looked back toward the car, something black and shiny slid out of the window, and I jumped in front of Preech. An explosion that sounded like a cannon hammered my ears, and I realized I'd been shot.

CHAPTER 23

Searing pain raced up my leg like someone had nailed me with a red-hot harpoon. It spun me backwards into Preech, and we crashed to the ground.

The smallest move I made hurt so bad my whole body quivered. My chest was tight and it got hard to breathe, like someone set an anvil on my chest.

The world started to shrink to a tiny white bubble. Preech held my head in his lap, and even though I could feel his hot breath on my face, it sounded like he was yelling from the back of a deep cave.

A police siren pierced the air, and tires smoked as the car next to us peeled out and took off. The squad car screeched to a stop where the other car had been, and Officer Duncan jumped out. "We got another unit comin' to nab those guys. What happened?"

I tried to talk, but the pain squeezed my throat shut. Preech's voice cracked and tears streamed down his face. "We were just standin' here and some psycho shot him...is he gonna die?"

Officer Shipley ran to me with a first aid kit and pointed to my leg. "Are you hit?"

I looked down at my leg and wondered why blood wasn't spurting out of it like a fountain. Normally, I would have been embarrassed to show the whole world my Scooby Doo underwear, but I gritted my teeth as I eased my jeans down. I expected to see blood, bits of bones, and ripped up meat where my leg used to be, but there wasn't a drop of blood. Instead a ruby red mark in the perfect shape of a cross was on my leg like a tattoo.

"Saved by the cross," Preech whispered as he pulled the iron cross out of my pocket. A fresh skid mark gleamed where the bullet had ricocheted off of it.

"Wow, that's gonna hurt for a long time," whistled Officer Shipley. "Did they get you anywhere else? Is your leg broke?"

"Nope, I can move it." I rolled my ankle back and forth, and even though it hurt like crazy, I was relieved that my leg still worked. There was a weird metallic twang in the back of my throat, like I'd sucked on an old penny.

"Well, before things get dicey, I suggest we get going. It's one heck of a long walk outta here boys, but the invite to ride in the squad car is still good if y'all want it," Officer Duncan said.

Preech wiped the tears off of his face with his tee shirt. "Oh, thank you. That would be excellent."

The officers pulled me up by my arms, and Preech hiked my jeans up, then opened the door as I limped into the back seat.

"You boys gonna tell us what would cause you to pull a stunt like that?"

"Well, if we knew what Rudy was doing—hold on, Rudy! Please pull around back, that's where our buddy went."

"We can't stay long. The alley there is a perfect place for an ambush, and I think the natives are gettin' restless around here."

We pulled around to the back of Larry's, and I felt tears burn the back of my eyes when I couldn't see him anywhere. All I saw were piles of trash and some men asleep on the heaps. One of them was using a brown head of lettuce for a pillow.

Officer Duncan looked around then back at us. "No dice, boys. Maybe he got smart and headed home."

Preech shook his head. "But that ain't like Rudy. Maybe he's inside, or in trouble around here somewhere."

"Well, we'll have one of the other units come look around. We gotta get your buddy looked at." The officer put the car in reverse and punched the gas as we flew backwards out of the alley.

He hit the siren a few times to make a way through the crowd that had formed during the mayhem, then zoomed down the street.

As we got to the old man next to the building, Officer Duncan pulled the cruiser to the curb. "Hey, did you see some knucklehead kid head ride his bike outta here?"

The man blinked himself awake and shielded the sun from his face with his dirty palm. "Ain't seen one leave, but seen three of them come in on bikes earlier. I bet myself a beer they'd never make it out."

"Well, we're takin' two of 'em back now. If you see the other one, light a match under him and tell him to get home immediately."

The man saluted Officer Duncan and settled back against the building. "Will do, Copper."

Officer Shipley turned to look at me. "How you doin? We gotta file a report on this but can swing you by the hospital first if we need to."

It still hurt, but I was able to wiggle all my toes again. "It's a little better, sir. If we go the station first, do y'all think you can find somethin' out about Rudy?"

"Yeah, we can get on the horn and see if there's any word. Maybe we can scare up some ice to put on your leg while we're there."

We pulled up to the dumpy gray building, and the officers helped me out of the car and into a chair in the small reception area. Officer Shipley grinned and pointed to my leg, "Don't go anywhere." Officer Duncan laughed as they walked down the long hall that led to the back of the building.

Preech had turned white as a flounder's belly. "Kevin, this is bad. This is real, real bad. Number one, Rudy may be gone forever. Number two, I ain't cut out for prison...I'll crack, I just know it."

I noticed that both of his eyes were about to crank into maximum twitch mode, and I got scared he was going to have a stroke or something. "Whoa. What do you mean prison? Did we break the law or somethin'?"

Preech gulped back a sob. "Nope, but we're at the police station. The next step is a trial, then jail...like on Kojak."

I thought they only took adults to prison and realized that getting shot and arrested did not make me feel any more man-like. If anything, I felt like I'd somehow taken a step backwards.

"Hey Preech buddy, I think they have to let us call a lawyer or something. You're good at talkin', and I'm sure everything's gonna be all rig—"

An ear-splitting yell echoed down the hall. "Do what? They did what? Do they have manure for brains?"

My mouth dropped open as a man almost as wide as the hallway stomped out of a door and stormed towards us faster than I'd ever seen a huge man move.

Pieces of brown gunk flew around the unlit cigar he chomped on as he screamed.

He stopped a few feet from us, and his voice growled like a full-throttle boat engine. "What in the heck we're y'all doin' down there? Did y'all get kicked in the head by a donkey and go stupid or somethin'? Talk to me. Now!"

I tried to speak, but my body throbbed and my mouth wouldn't work. My leg had hurt too bad to cry before, but I felt like a dam of tears was about to bust.

I looked at Preech and his eyelids were going so crazy I thought he was going to take off like an airplane.

Officer Shipley handed me a bag of ice and a glass of water. After I took a sip, I put the ice bag on my leg and cleared my throat. "Well, ummm, it was like—"

Then a sound like an eighteen wheeler smashing into a glass factory exploded all around us. The officers jumped behind desks, and Preech sat there and blinked.

I looked in the direction of the crash, and my heart took off like a flying fish. It was Rudy sitting on his bike. He was covered in sweat and looked like he'd taken a shower with his clothes on. When he saw me, he smiled so big his good eye pinched shut.

I glanced down and saw the brick he'd thrown through the plate-glass window, and noticed his address was written on it.

Rudy yelled, "Hey there! I live on Elm, remember?" Then I blinked and he had disappeared.

Officer Duncan pointed at us. "Hey, you two know where he lives. Get in the car and show me. Pronto."

I held the bag of ice to my chest like a baby and put my arm around Preech's shoulders to help me back into the cruiser.

Officer Duncan ran past us and jumped in the driver's seat. As I shut the door, he punched the gas so hard I thought his foot was going to go through the floorboard.

We flew down the streets, but I knew Rudy would have used the yards and alleys to get there way faster.

Preech leaned over and whispered, "Man, this is even worse. If Ted's in town and hears what we did, Rudy's a goner."

I whispered back, "Did you see him on his bike? I'm thinkin' he's got a plan. He wouldn't have broken the window and got every cop in town buzzed up like hornets if he didn't."

Only one of Preech's eyes twitched, so I figured he was getting better. "Okay, but I wish he'd told us what's goin' on. This has turned into the worst day ever, and it feels like I've been ridin' a roller coaster with a blindfold on."

"I know buddy, me too."

The police car turned onto Rudy's street, and the first thing I noticed was his bike parked way out in the yard next to the street. He usually parked it in the garage, but I thought he might have left it out as a beacon.

The car screeched to a stop, and Officer Duncan jumped out and ran to the front door. Preech slung my arm over his shoulder, then eased me out as quickly as he could. We watched Officer Duncan pound on the door, then heard a scream from the back of the house.

Rudy's scream.

Preech leaned over and tapped his back for me to get on, then ran around the house with me hanging on like a monkey. He skidded to a stop at the fence, and set me down as he pointed towards the yard. Rudy stood in the middle of it, and Ted faced him with a baseball bat in one hand and a bottle of whiskey in the other.

Officer Duncan pushed past us as he opened the gate and ran through. Ted was yelling so loud at Rudy I doubted he heard Officer Duncan come up behind him. Officer Duncan grabbed Ted's shoulder, and Ted spun around and smashed his elbow into the officer's mouth. The policeman staggered back a few steps, then melted into a heap on the grass.

Ted stared down at the fallen officer and screamed, "Great, now there'll be two bodies I have to bury."

A deep voice echoed through the backyard. It was deep and strong. And almost manly. "Stop it Ted. Now."

I looked at Preech, and when I saw the shocked look on his face I realized the voice had come from me.

Ted looked at me and shook his head. He took a swig of whiskey, then hurled the bottle at us. I felt the wind off of it as it missed my head by a couple of inches and exploded against the house.

His stare was evil, and it bored right into my brain. As he came towards me he growled, "I never liked you two useless maggots. I'm gonna smash you up real good for that smart mouth."

I felt Preech pull my shirt, but even if I could run, something told me I had to do something. I reached into my pocket and realized the knives were gone. My fingers found something round and jagged, and I pulled out my lucky rock.

Ted was ten steps away when I wound my arm back and threw the rock harder than I'd ever thrown anything in my life.

The rock zipped from my fingers and smashed Ted right in the middle of his forehead. It sounded like a golf ball bouncing off a fence.

Ted stopped in his tracks, and stood still for a couple of seconds. Blood started as a trickle, then turned into a mini-waterfall as it gushed down his face.

He let out a sound like a wounded bear, then ran and swung the bat at us as he tried to wipe his eyes clean. Preech and I hit the dirt, and the bat exploded when it hit the fence. Sharp shards of wood peppered us as we laid on the ground.

I looked up to see Officer Shipley standing next to me, gritting his teeth and pulling the black club off of his belt. "Drop the weapon and get face down on the grass."

Ted grunted as he swung the jagged half-bat at the officer, who leaned back just enough for the bat to miss him. The force of the swing turned Ted sideways, and the officer reached over the fence and clobbered Ted in the back of the head with his club. Ted's knees buckled, and he fell to the grass like a bag of hammers.

Rudy cheered and ran towards us, and Officer Shipley cuffed Ted then ran to Officer Duncan.

Just as Rudy passed Ted, he snapped his fingers and skidded to a stop. He did a quick look around to make sure no one was watching, then quickly reached into his pocket and pulled out a wadded up envelope. Rudy jammed it in Ted's back pocket then jumped over him.

Preech put one of my arms over his shoulder as Rudy got under the other. Preech's smile had more teeth than I knew he had. "Kev man, I've read David and Goliath like a hundred times. That was awesome!"

Daisy ran out of the house and hugged the three of us, and I noticed she had a black eye like Rudy's. The other policemen surrounded Ted and cuffed his ankles before they stood him up.

As they emptied his pockets, one of the officers opened the envelope. His eyes bugged out as he looked through the papers, and he called another policeman to take a look.

The other officer read them, then waved the papers in Ted's face. "Scumbags like you make me sick. Don't you know havin' somethin' like this is treason?"

Ted grunted and spit in the grass. "Somethin' like what? I ain't never seen that stuff before."

"Well, it's got your name and address on it. And if I ain't mistakin', it's materials for a nuclear bomb and some return address in Russia. With havin' assaulted an officer of the law and dealin' with the enemy, you ain't gonna see the light of day for a long, long time."

"It ain't mine," screamed Ted as they pushed him towards the cruisers.

Officer Duncan was behind the other policemen. He held his jaw with one hand and pointed to us with the other. "You know boys, I hear there's a fella in the Flats that's a whiz at makin' perfectly legal-lookin' documents. Y'all wouldn't know anything about that, would ya?"

We shook our heads.

"Well, I'm gonna let the justice system do its thing with that Ted fella. I'm tellin' you now that if I ever see y'all even pointin' your bikes that direction again, I'm gonna run you three up the flagpole myself. Got it?"

Preech clasped his hands together and bowed to the officer. "Sir, my solemn promise to you is that you will never, ever, ever have to worry about that."

Rudy and I nodded, and Officer Duncan walked to his cruiser.

As the policemen finished their reports and left for their cars, one walked up with my lucky rock in his hand. "This appears to have done a number on that big fella. Where'd you get it?"

I opened my palm for the officer to give it to me and hoped they wouldn't have to keep it for evidence. "From my pocket, sir. Can I please have it back?"

He smiled and sat it in my hand. "No, what I meant was did you get it at one of those crazy novelty stores? I've seen a lot of gold and diamonds in this line of work, and if I didn't know any better, I'd swear that was the largest black diamond I've ever touched."

Rudy started to say something but Preech stomped him on the foot. "Oh, yeah, it was at one of those stores in the mall. They got tons of 'em."

The officer looked at us and smiled, then patted me on the back and walked to his car.

Preech waited for the policeman to get out of earshot, then grinned at me and Rudy. "There were piles of those around the shipwreck, and I guarantee you they didn't have fake diamonds when that ship went down. We're rich!"

"Dangit," Rudy said as he grabbed his hair with his fists. "I can't remember where I put mine."

I was about to tell him that we'd help him look for it when I heard car tires screech to a stop in front of the house. It was my mom and dad, and suddenly I wished I was back in Florida. From the looks on their faces, something told me I'd be safer under water with the shark.

CHAPTER 24

Three weeks later we were back on Oliver's porch. For the first time ever, it was us who told the story and Oliver who sat wide-eyed and listened.

After we finished, he shook his head and pointed to Rudy. "First thing, I wish you woulda told me about what y'all were up to, but since things ended like they did, I reckon' it was best you didn't. Second, remember you can choose your actions, but not what happens. Third, every time you see a soldier or a policeman, you shake their hand, look 'em in the eye, and thank 'em for what they do."

We nodded, and Preech pulled his lucky rock out of his pocket and stared at it. "Since we've been grounded until today and couldn't go anywhere but school and home, it's been drivin' me nuts to know if these are real. Do you know where we can take them, Oliver?"

He smiled and looked at his yard. "Yep, I know a fella who can tell us. Now that y'all told me what the officer said, I reckon I better pick mine out of my rock garden there and put it up somewhere safe."

I pulled my lucky rock out of my pocket and watched the sunlight dance across it. "Do you think we can go back to the shipwreck and get the rest of 'em? If they turn out to be real?"

Oliver grinned. "You betcha, especially since y'all ain't grounded any more. How was lock-down for you, Kevin?"

166

"Horrible. Once my leg got better, my folks told me I had to do anything Milly wanted to. I have like fifty layers of nail polish on my toes, and I don't think it will ever come off."

Oliver laughed and looked at Rudy. "How'd yours go?"

"Not bad at all. I went with my mom to sign the divorce papers, and we got to hang out without Ted around. One cool thing was that my aunt came down and we—"

Preech interrupted Rudy, "Oh yeah, that reminds me. I almost forgot about the weirdest thing ever. Lemme go get somethin'." Preech dropped his lucky rock in his pocket and ran to his bike.

Rudy scowled at Preech and continued, "Anyway, she came down and we threw Ted's stuff away and repainted the house. It's a million times better."

Oliver patted him on the shoulder. "Well, I don't reckon we'll have to worry about Ted. I talked to a friend of mine that's a judge, and he said they're gonna nail him good."

Preech pulled a magazine from the pile of stuff on his bike. "Got it," he yelled as he ran and jumped back on the porch. "My grandmother went to Europe and brought me this and some other stuff. I couldn't read all the words, but I think it says something about how things are different now since the war."

Oliver adjusted his glasses as Preech opened the magazine and handed it to him. Preech pointed to the necklace on a lady in the picture. "The freaky thing is that she has a dog tag that looks just like yours."

Oliver looked at the picture, then sat back in his chair so hard it almost snapped in half. "It's her. It's Marlena. My Marlena...my wife." Oliver's voice cracked. "She's alive. Holy cow she's alive. When did your gramma get this?"

Preech scratched his head. "A month or so ago when she was there. It can't be too old.

Oliver rubbed his fingers on the picture like he was touching a real person. "The diamonds waited a hundred years or so, so they're gonna have to wait a little bit longer. We're goin' after a bigger treasure." Oliver hugged the magazine to his chest as a grin slid across his face.

He raised his cane like a Civil War general charging into battle. "Saddle up posse, we're headin' to Germany!"

ACKNOWLEDGEMENTS

There is no way to put into words my gratitude for all of the support—and bare-knuckled, between the eyes critiques—that ultimately made me a better writer and helped make *Lucky Rocks* a better experience.

In no particular order: Thanks to Mom and Dad (for teaching us to love reading), Jen, Annie, Max, Lena, Andrea, John, Trilby (for all of the time and excellent, eagle-eye catches that helped keep me from looking like an idiot!), Meridith, Clay, Gretchen, Todd, Bill, and all of my crit partners in real life and cyber space: Muffet, Bill, Laney, Patricia, Nancy, Cynthia, Lori, Brenda, Bridgette, and Tahni. A special double thanks to Mary Bill (because that sweet, sweet lady combed it through twice and gave me excellent advice both times). Thanks to internet whiz Cindy, graphics wizard Nathan, the "Mom and Son" teams of Nicole and Cade as well as Lori and Julien, the "Father and Son" teams of Darron and Mason, Granville and Austin (and Caroline), Trent and Jacob, Rob and Roman, Eddie and Edwin, Christy, Juli, Jessica, Ryan, Jill, Kirk, Anita, Bryan, Dr. Jeff H., Jourdin, Blanca, Michael, Betty, Eric, Chris, Matt, Doug, Paul, Jeff, all of the excellent librarians at the Dallas Public Library and the fine folks at Ten Story Books for believing in me.

And a huge thank you to everyone involved with the Society of Children's Book Writers and Illustrators, the most helpful and organized group of dreamers I've ever met.

It took a village, and I appreciate all of the help and encouragement.

ABOUT THE AUTHOR

From the first second I held a fishing pole, I was hooked. To this day, I can't pass a body of water without wondering what kind of fish (or bait) is cruising around in it. I also love a good joke, and playing jokes on people—which is why I rarely answer my phone or open email around April Fool's day!

I graduated from the University of Texas with a degree in Journalism, and once heard a really smart person say "Readers are Leaders." I hope you agree.

Please visit my website at www.murrayrichter.com.

60410295R00106

Made in the USA
Middletown, DE
21 August 2019